P9-CAF-275

Whittlesworth
Comes to Christmas

Whittlesworth
Comes to Christmas

For the Boerner Family,

Gerald R. Toner

Good friends who know the value
of family and the spirit of Christmas!
Wishing you all my very best for
a Merry Christmas, 1991!

Jerry Toner
12/10/91
Louisville

Pelican Publishing Company
Gretna 1991

Copyright © 1991
By Gerald R. Toner
All rights reserved

Toner, Gerald R.
    Whittlesworth comes to Christmas / Gerald R. Toner.
       p.   cm.
    ISBN 0-88289-877-9
    I. Title.
PS3570.0484W48   1991
813′.54—dc20

91-23134
CIP

Illustrations by Joyce Haynes

Manufactured in the United States of America

Published by Pelican Publishing Company, Inc.
1101 Monroe Street, Gretna, Louisiana 70053

*For every family and every home—my own
included—and for every soul that yearns to
come home but lacks the means
and
in memory of Gussie,
whose endless capacity to give
and receive love will never be forgotten*

Contents

Preface

Whittlesworth Comes to Christmas has a history which, in itself, would comprise a modest epic of a novel or motion picture. The basic plot was first developed almost twenty-four years ago in a very short story which appeared in a high-school publication. Around ten years ago I came across the original version while straightening up some old papers in my attic, and decided to resurrect the tale. I composed a novella, which saw several drafts and by the mid-1980s was rendered to a clean, manuscript form.

On the urging of my friend, Leo Burmester, a stage and film actor, *Whittlesworth* became a screenplay. It was eventually represented by another Kentuckian, Peter Franklin, who tried unsuccessfully for two years or so to pique Hollywood's interest. Even as this nation's homeless, urban, and family crises increased, no one was interested in an unknown writer's whimsical Christmas tale.

Then came Pelican and the success of *Lipstick Like Lindsay's and Other Christmas Stories. Whittlesworth* again called and I rewrote the entire novella from beginning to end, altering characters, story line, and mood to fit my current vision.

Over the past twenty years I would chafe—as writers

9

do with great regularity—every time another hobo Christmas story would surface on television. My only consolation was that *Whittlesworth* was its own tale long before those other stories existed, and would stand or fall on its own merit. After all, the original Christmas story was about an itinerant, out-of-work carpenter who slept under viaducts and spent far more time with disparate and troubled families than with giddily happy ones.

In the end, *Whittlesworth* hopefully speaks to every family where divorce, death, and debts threaten that family's very survival. The characters in this novel are far from perfect Christmas types. They have their flaws and their problems, and without each other they could hope only to subsist and survive. As a family unit—even while occasionally at one another's throats—the magical potential for triumph arises.

Acknowledgments

When Whittlesworth first came to life more than twenty years ago, my friend Charles Edward ("Chuck") Pogue was present as its illustrator. In later years as an actor, Chuck would repeat his affection for the old tale and we would bemoan the passing of the Dickensian style in modern writing and the Capra-esque quality in modern films. During the past six months, Chuck, now an accomplished screenwriter, has pitched around numerous points—broad and fine—which have helped *Whittlesworth* approach the storytelling standards of Dickens and Capra (note that I say "approach" rather than "attain"). My thanks to him for twenty-some years of criticism. It finally brought Whittlesworth to maturity.

Thanks also to Leo Burmester and Peter Franklin, who preserved my faith in this story. To helpful critics along the way: Liz Dahl; Ned Beatty; my editor, John Rogers; Pelican's president, Dr. Milburn Calhoun; my steady friend Steve Vinsavich; and my wife, Carol. May you all enjoy the final product more than you did delivering to me the criticisms of its forerunners!

11

CHAPTER 1

Katie's Epistle

KATIE'S EYES OPENED with the first gong of the big mantelpiece clock downstairs. She counted five more. She knew she was the first one awake, but still she listened just to be sure. On any ordinary morning she would have slept right through the clock's off-key, low bass clunking. But this morning was hardly ordinary.

Everything was different about this morning. The house itself seemed alive. Joists creaked slightly with the growing cold, their muffled cries circulating within plaster walls and ceilings and thickly beamed oak floors. She could hear the steady thump, thump, thump of the cavernous gas furnace as it struggled to raise the temperature within the drafty mansion to a respectable 68 degrees. The slight rattle of windowpanes as the wind passed by the house from the stormy west sent a message to Katie, urging her faintly to take action.

Katie listened carefully, trying to detect the sound of stirring humans over the whispers of the house. There was no one up and about. She was sure of that. Except for the times when her mother seemed particularly agitated, when she got up and made coffee and smoked cigarettes and walked around the house in her bathrobe long before

13

the dawn, no one was ever up by six. Certainly not her grandmother—who awoke exactly at seven, never fail.

Slipping into the furry slippers and flannel robe her grandmother had given her last Christmas, Katie softly shuffled rather than lifted her feet as she moved through the upstairs hall. She couldn't afford any extra sounds—no supplements to the creaking, thumping, and rattling which might alert her mother or grandmother that she was up. She sneaked down the hallway, passing her mother's and then her grandmother's room. She paused and peered at the never-slumbering gaze of her family's ancestors, portrayed in a hundred and fifty years of variant clothing styles on the hallway's walls. It was a stern and formidable army to confront in the gray moments before dawn, but a confrontation that she somehow felt was necessary.

Katie reached the top step and peered through the spindles to the hallway below. Where just the night before there had been the bright, blinding brightness of the front hall chandelier there was now darkness. Where there had been loud voices there was total silence.

"Out of the question." Katie had been awakened by the sousaphone voice of her great uncle Thaddeus. What was out of the question? She tiptoed down to perch at the last curve in the stairs—just as she was now doing—and like an audience implanted high within the gallery seats, watched the drama that was being enacted in the front entranceway below.

"We're happy here!" her grandmother's voice responded to something else Thaddeus had said. Then very clearly came Thaddeus's voice again.

"Since John died I've looked after you and Jane and even Katie. There's only one way I can continue to do that . . . at least in the way John would've wanted it."

"Thad, your sacrifice and generosity is truly a thing of wonder." Her mother's low voice was unmistakable. It seemed to reflect the mocking knowledge that something was funny—a sort of private joke that she would never reveal willingly to anyone. Thaddeus tossed the comment aside.

"Say what you will, Jane. I promised you both that I'd share some of the profit with you when the deal's over, and I meant it. But the only way I can continue to do what I know John would've wanted done—namely keeping you all safe and secure—is to get you out of this neighborhood!"

"You didn't feel compelled to keep us safe and secure when Dad was alive. Why worry about it now?"

"Now is the first time in more than fifty years that I have both the power and the means to salvage what little wealth this family has preserved!"

"That's it, isn't it? You finally got the marbles all to yourself, now that Dad's gone."

"Jane . . . that's too harsh," Helen's voice interrupted.

"No, that's all right. Control? Sure. I want it. Anyone who seeks to effect change in this world wants it. Whether the change is good or bad is for the historians. I think my idea is a good one. One that will preserve this part of the city for the good of everyone."

"You're not in front of the Chamber of Commerce, Uncle Thad. Cut out the 'it's a tough job, but someone has to do it' routine."

"Jane, just *once*, try being a little more open in your thinking. Besides, you're not any recognized authority on making big plans work out."

"Thaddeus . . . I'll ignore the implications that last remark is supposed to convey. It's just that I've heard that the project could be better."

"And who, may I ask, is your source for this brainstorm?"

"Well, Peter. . . ." Jane's voice trailed off. She never spoke of Peter very much in Katie's presence. Katie wondered why, but knew somehow not to ask.

"Peter O'Malley? Again?" Now it was Thaddeus's voice that sounded as if it were communicating some insider's joke. "That young man doesn't know which end of his pencil to sharpen! Every public meeting he's come to he's been a source of disruption. If he had joined the Plan instead of carping about it at every turn, he might have made a contribution. But every idea he's had has been without support or any figures to back it up!"

"Give him a chance!"

Thad drew back in mock surprise. "You're telling *me* to give him a chance?" Katie strained to hear something more—something that would explain what he meant. Instead, his words were like missing pieces of a puzzle. The parts of their collective whole seemed to be known to everyone except Katie.

Thaddeus's voice grew calm. "Helen. Jane. Listen to reason on this thing. This place is falling down around you. The neighborhood's too far gone. It's dead. I mean, after all, the house is mine; I should know what it would cost to repair."

"I thought your mother left the family's holdings to all three of her sons equally." Jane's voice was crystalline now—no smoky murmurs, no touch of indecision. It carried the edge of the reporter, probing for truth.

Katie had strained to listen. It was like one of those questions on her grandmother's quiz shows, hanging out in mid-air, stumping the fellow who had been winning everything in sight. Thaddeus was flustered. Katie could tell by the way he flung his overcoat over his arm instead of answering.

"Well?" Jane implicitly repeated her question. "You don't own the house or the rest of the family property outright, do you?"

"It was left to the brothers equally . . . survivor take all. You know that!"

"I know. That's not what I mean, Thad."

Thaddeus turned a bright red, his ears practically aflame. "Whittlesworth will sign off on the house *and* the Plan," he said.

"So! Uncle Whittlesworth hasn't signed off yet! You see, mother, that's what's got him nervous. He doesn't have it all nailed down."

"Details. Minor details. Whittlesworth hasn't shown any interest in any of us since before I was born. As far as I'm concerned, he's not even real!"

"I'll bet he's real enough to stop your Plan if he wants to. And it looks to me like he's real enough to have you running scared."

Helen had listened in silent frustration, trying at times to interject throughout the exchange. She finally shook her head and started for the stairs. "You two go on arguing if you like. Whit Ash left my life far too long ago to even think about that man again! I'm going to bed!" Helen started up the stairs and Katie instinctively withdrew into the shadows. A stair tread creaked. Thaddeus and Jane continued to argue while Helen softly directed her voice towards the top of the stairs. "Katie Ash . . . you go to bed. I know you're up there."

Katie had retreated silently to her room, where she had crawled under the big down comforter her grandma had used as a little girl. She had strained to hear her great uncle Thaddeus's final words, but the floors, ceilings, and walls were too thick. The voices of Thaddeus and her mother had become a jumble of sounds, like the tune of a vaguely familiar song, until eventually Thaddeus could be heard distinctly shouting, "Good night, then!"

The door had slammed and Katie had turned over, pondering the many interpretations of what had just transpired and what had been happening—unspoken but sensed—for several months. It concerned their home (well, her grandmother's home), some sort of Plan that her great uncle Thaddeus wanted very much, and finally the mention of the mysterious Whittlesworth.

Whittlesworth. He was more like a ghost than her second great uncle. Once or twice his name had been mentioned by her grandfather. They had been brothers and playmates. Once, her grandfather had cried while he was talking about him. When her Grandpa John had his heart attack and everyone was coming back into town for the funeral, she had heard Whittlesworth mentioned again. They thought he might finally come back. He hadn't. She had heard her mother talk about being "as rich as Whittlesworth" a few times. That was it. Nothing more. Nothing that would translate from the realm of legend into the habitat of the real. She knew more about Santa Claus than Whittlesworth! It was this final thought that had formed her resolution the night before.

Now Katie crept down the long stairway, her hand sliding carefully along the broad mahogany banister. She stopped at the bottom of the stair and listened to make sure that no one had heard her descent. There was just the faint rattling of the large front door as the wind blew.

She turned into the front parlor and began to pass the unlit Christmas tree, stopped, thought for a moment, knelt at the foot of the tree, and plugged it in. The little spruce burst into a crazy quilt of bright lights. Katie leaned back, caught up in its beauty, forgetting for a moment her main purpose. It was like Christmas morning without the distraction of presents or adults. It was even better in some ways, since Christmas was still almost two weeks away. The holiday wasn't over; it was just beginning.

Something or someone stirred upstairs. Katie refocused on the business at hand. She stood up, went to the tall Victorian secretary which had belonged to her grandfather, and moved the captain's chair out far enough to stand on it and reach the compartments above the desk's leather top. One after the other she searched the pigeonholes for the book she would need. It was brown leather with gold lettering, and it was all in tatters. Katie probed and poked her way through one slot after another until the old book emerged. She took it down, removed a piece of stationery from the neighboring compartment, and started turning each page of the address book carefully. Two pages—yellowed by time and faded to near invisibility—bore the name "Ash." She followed from her mother's name, tracing backwards through a history recorded in black, blue, and the oldest—green—ink. Names which didn't mean a thing to her were predominant. Many were scratched through and rewritten with different addresses. Some were just scratched through.

All of it was very confusing—even for a bright six-year-old like Katie. For a moment she thought her entire mission might be wasted. Then she saw it. It was his first name that had confused her: James Whittlesworth Ash. He had always simply been called "Whittlesworth"—an old family name, as her grandfather had explained it. The "James" part was new to her. Katie wondered for a moment whether she should call him Great Uncle James. Then she decided it was better not to confuse him. He was probably used to being called "Uncle Whittlesworth."

Katie took a pen from the odd bunch of Savings & Loan ballpoints and tortoise-shell fountain pens stuffed into a tarnished silver cup. She thought for a second, composing her thoughts, and then began. One by one she carefully printed each word so that he would be sure to be able to read it.

Dear Uncle Whittlesworth:

We have never met. I am your great niece, Katie. My mother is your niece. I was named for your mother. My family does not talk about you much. My Grandpa John did. But only to me. He really loved you. He died last year. Did anyone tell you? Christmas is two weeks away. Can you come? You can stay in my room. I will sleep on the couch. I hope you can come.

Love,

KATIE ASH

Katie carefully and precisely folded her letter in three segments, addressed an envelope, licked and planted a stamp, then crept quietly to the front door. She twisted the latch and turned the large brass handle as she pulled the ten-foot door towards her. Stepping out into the cold December air, she clipped her letter to the clothespin which her Grandmother kept attached to the mailbox and, shivering, withdrew into the warmth of the house.

She closed the door behind her, relatched it, and breathed a sigh of relief. Success! So far, anyway. The letter was done and almost sent. Katie crossed her fingers, closed her eyes, and made a quick wish. Please come, she thought.

CHAPTER 2

Thaddeus's Letter

THADDEUS EDWARD ASH, who had never been a major player in the game of life, stood on the brink of prominence. He was arriving a bit late perhaps, but not too late. He paced from one end of his newly panelled and expanded office to the other. No one had needed John's office, so he had knocked the wall out.

Things were finally happening. Forces were at work. He could feel them, like an energy flow coursing through him. They were good forces—the Plan he had been laboring over for years, the coalition of civic leaders and power brokers he had gathered and manipulated with the dexterity of a diplomat, the remaining fortunes of his own family. But there were also bad, or at least misguided, forces—Jane, Helen, and the loose-knit opposition which peripatetically raised their disjointed voices against the Plan. The very people who were most likely to benefit from change! Life was not predictable.

A glimmer of light caught his eye. It was either the late afternoon sun or the glint from the new recessed lighting which ringed his office; he couldn't tell. But it drew his attention to the two portraits on the new back wall, and he smiled. He had never before appreciated the irony of

Sally's bright and mesmerizing image portrayed beside the old-fashioned, formal pose of his dead brother, John.

Sally was the future. She was young—not yet forty. She was bright, shrewd, full of innovative concepts and unique ways of examining very ordinary circumstances. Some might even say Ash Square Development was her progeny as much as it was Thaddeus's. Beside her image hung the past in the persona of John Joseph Ash. In his youth Thaddeus had admired John—even looked up to him as a figure to emulate. Then Thaddeus had seen one opportunity after another slip away from them. Forever the baby brother, he had watched the family's fortune ebb decade after decade. Then the Plan had come forth from Sally and himself, and with it the opportunity to turn the family's future around.

John had died fighting Ash Square Development. And why? Thaddeus still wasn't sure. He was fairly confident that John's first reason must have been strictly selfish and sentimental: the wrecking ball was set for the old family mansion, and John had lived there all his life. Thaddeus could appreciate that. He wasn't without feelings.

John had also contended that the building and its adjoining grounds were historic, and that the city needed to recall and respect its heritage, but Thaddeus suspected that it was just John's excuse for burying his head in the past. Thaddeus had been wise enough to move out of the city and into the suburbs thirty years before. City dwelling held no charm for him. The fact that his grandfather had built the house was of underwhelming significance.

A third explanation for John's intransigence had to be his oft-repeated rubric that: "You just can't put all of those people out of their homes. Even if we *do* own the property, it's just not right." John had said that so many times that it ran like a warped record in Thaddeus's mind. John could simply never see that the people who still lived on Park Place Drive would be much happier in the relocation housing the mayor had promised them. No more steps for the older people, better security for the single women, and a nice new playground for the kids. All of this was undeniably true, yet John had died resisting the future.

Thaddeus pushed the buzzer on his phone, summoning his secretary, then wandered over to the model of Ash Square Development which occupied the northwest corner of his office. It was like a fantastic toy on the verge of springing to life—a Pinocchio for grown men. It was fine. In fact, it was almost exquisite . . . *where* was Miss Pierce?

Thaddeus spun around and, mashing down the bar on his intercom, called her this time. Still no answer. Whenever he needed her she was in the bathroom or getting coffee or down the hall. Kindness was one thing, but slavery to incompetence was another. Perhaps the Thaddeus of three years ago would have tolerated these vagaries. The *new* Thaddeus would never let such sloth go unpunished.

Miss Pierce appeared in the door just as Thaddeus was muttering, "I'll just go ahead and fire her after the New Year!" Thaddeus looked up.

"I called you twice."

"I'm sorry, Mr. Ash. I was checking on that attorney's home phone number you asked me for."

"Er . . . yes." Thaddeus had forgotten the assignment he had sworn was paramount just ten minutes before. Miss Pierce had been John's secretary before she had started working for him. Maybe it was just the question of her loyalty that bothered him. Either way, he still couldn't have an employee he was unsure of—for any reason.

"I'm still looking. I just wanted to tell you that your niece's friend is in the lobby and would like to see you."

It took Thaddeus a moment to make the nexus. His niece. Jane. Jane's "friend." She must mean O'Malley. Thaddeus frowned.

"What does that nitwit want?"

"He said there's been a misunderstanding about his plans for Ash Square Development."

"That young man is not only incompetent, he's obnoxious. The only misunderstandings are in his feeble brain." Thaddeus smiled. "Let him wait. Take a letter."

Miss Pierce obediently lowered herself into the client's chair situated at the edge of Thaddeus's glass-and-chrome desk. She disliked Thaddeus almost as much as she had adored John. It mystified her that the same parents could spawn two brothers who were so different. Thaddeus settled into his gray suede chair. He stared out the window at the city below. He could actually see the old mansion and Park Place Drive. His body tensed into one immobile hulk.

Thaddeus was frightened. It was not a fear that he could prevent or overcome by ignoring. He had ignored the problem for far too long. The crux of it all was Whittlesworth. After a lifetime of carrying one dimwit, idealistic older brother along, the prospect of now dealing with another, more renowned eccentric was bothersome at the very least. What if Whittlesworth, the family hermit, was as crazy as John and refused to sign off on the Plan? The proposition was unthinkable, but he had been plagued by that very proposition for the past several weeks.

Thaddeus had known from the Plan's first day that Whittlesworth's signature had to appear on the deed and closing documents—presuming his older brother lived until year's end. He had read tabloid rumors of Whittlesworth's ill health with increasing interest over the past six months, gambling on the chance that when December came, Whittlesworth would be long dead. Time and again Thaddeus had put off contacting the family wild card, hoping that when the time arrived he would be securely shuffled back into the deck. Thus far, Whittlesworth had not obliged.

"Did you want to dictate a letter, Mr. Ash?" Miss Pierce's voice startled Thaddeus. He fumbled for a moment.

"Yes," he finally said, sitting upright, "to Mr. James Whittlesworth Ash . . . "

"Your brother?" Miss Pierce practically fell out of the chair.

"Yes . . . and not a word to anyone. Do you understand?"

"Yes, of course, Mr. Ash."

Thaddeus wondered if she was thinking about her year-end termination. He certainly didn't want her to go around blabbing about this. His voice became silky, ameliorative.

"You know, Margaret, the old man may be as nutty as they all say, but he must have been a helluva business man in his day. This city ought to have at least his tacit cooperation if we're to get the Plan off the ground."

"Yes, Mr. Ash." Her voice seemed pleasant and agreeable, but Thaddeus had no doubts about her loyalties, especially now. She had been irrationally dedicated to John. Another problem for another day.

"Dear Brother." Thaddeus looked at his secretary with a condescending smile. "I think that will be the best way to begin. Dear Brother—it has been a long time since the family has heard from you. We received your check for John's funeral. It was certainly more than adequate. Your generosity was appreciated. Okay, next paragraph: With Christmas drawing near, I have a rather unique, two-fold request. First, we would ask that you reconsider your habit of solitude . . . " Thaddeus turned to Miss Pierce with a friendly tone. "Would you believe we've never seen the old man?"

"Yes, sir, that's part of his legend."

"Yes . . . so anyway, reconsider your habit of solitude and spend this Christmas with us. Secondly, we are preparing to . . . " Thaddeus contemplated the best way in which to gain his brother's silent support, "secure our futures—Helen's security being paramount—by redeveloping the family holdings with a plan that has gained broad-based support from the city, community, and . . . " Thaddeus contemplated the minor lie he was about to perpetrate, "the remaining family members. The immediate and long-term returns on investment will be substantial. Next paragraph: It will be necessary for you to execute the final deed for the transferral of property to Ash Square Development, Inc. For reasons related to the development team out of Houston, the closing will be scheduled for December 23. If you cannot attend, we will certainly understand. A restricted power of attorney is enclosed for your execution. Hoping this season finds you well. Sincerely . . . and so on and so forth. If you would, please get that typed immediately."

"Yes, sir." Margaret Pierce stood up and started for the door. "What about Mr. O'Malley?"

"Hmmm?" Thaddeus's mind was thousands of miles away, imagining the arrival of his simple letter at the guarded quarters of his reclusive older brother. "O'Malley? Oh, yes." His voice regained its snap. "Send him in. But let him know I only have a few minutes before my next appointment."

"But I believe your calendar is free . . . "

"Not for Peter O'Malley."

"Oh, I understand. I'll send him in right away."

Thaddeus stood up and paced to the model he had been admiring just moments before—the model of a dream which O'Malley and his fringe-element friends were opposing.

O'Malley bounded into the room with the energy normally reserved for collegians. He was nearing forty, well past the normal stage of starry-eyed idealism—more like a throwback to the sixties than a forward thinker of the nineties. Thaddeus despised him—despised him for his current status as a thorn in the flesh, despised him for the minor role he had played in Jane's life years earlier, and most of all despised him for his ineffectuality. Sure, he'd done a few splashy preservation projects ten years back, but everything O'Malley had designed since had either failed in the making or been impractical in the end result. If O'Malley had possessed even a minor track record, Thaddeus might have paid him at least perfunctory attention. As it was, he was just a bad penny returned.

"Hi, Thaddeus. Thought maybe you all had forgotten about me!" O'Malley was absurdly effervescent.

Thaddeus accepted O'Malley's outstretched hand with some hesitation. "No. We didn't forget about you. How could we?" Thaddeus laughed in an anemic attempt to appear good-natured. "I simply had some other business to attend to. Now, what can I do for you?"

"Thad, I'll get right to the point." Thaddeus always cringed when a lesser creature such as O'Malley called him by his family and club name. "I want you to reconsider my alternative for the Plan . . . "

"Out of the question." Thaddeus was ready for him, and his response was almost too eager. He took a breath and continued. "The plans are already set, Peter. Prepared, approved, and set! It's a little late now to be changing things."

"You told me a month ago that it was too early to make any changes."

"That was a month ago. Things have moved along more rapidly in the past few weeks."

"Thad, it's not too late to make changes until it's finished. Now, listen to me for a second . . . ." O'Malley launched into his now familiar litany of Plan amendments. It was a list straight out of a dreamer's textbook: Save the house. Develop the back alleys. Build "unobtrusive" underground parking. Relandscape the park. Restore amenity shopping for the neighborhood types.

O'Malley droned on. Save St. Andrew's from the wrecker's unkind ball . . .

"You know, the bishop fully approves of the Plan as it's currently drawn." Thaddeus couldn't allow this point to go unchallenged. O'Malley seemed to possess the profound belief that the world ran or should run according to the misguided dictates of him and his friends—St. Andrew's James Spencer chief among them—rather than the dictates of any higher authority.

"Yes, but if the committee would just examine the designs which I've drawn . . . "

"Peter . . . you are a fine architect. Some have called you gifted. But you are not the architect on this project. The firm from Chicago was selected by Cartwright. If they had selected you . . . "

"I'll bet *that* was never an option."

Thaddeus's eyes narrowed. Enough common courtesies. "Would you have expected them to choose a one-man show . . . with your track record?"

O'Malley's exuberance flagged. "If I had proposed the better preliminary plan."

"Exactly. The word 'if' is a very important one. In the judgment of the principals, you did not submit the better preliminary plan. Subject closed."

The muscles in O'Malley's jaw set. He had heard all of these excuses before. He took one step closer to Thaddeus and his model for Ash Square Development. They stood facing each other over the miniature skyline.

"Let's not waste any more time, Thad." Again Thaddeus winced. O'Malley made his feelings clear with a dismissive sweep of his hand over the intricate model laid out before him. "We see this thing two different ways. I won't take up your time anymore and don't you take up mine. Jane has asked me to represent her interests during the final committee meetings . . . "

Thaddeus cut O'Malley off. "I would think, based only on any sensitivity you have remaining, and any common decency you may have ever possessed, that you would not interpose Jane into these matters."

"My relationship with Jane is my business."

"I would say, Peter, that some time ago you made sure that it was *not* your business."

O'Malley ignored the comment. "I'll see you at the meetings."

"I warn you. Disrupt this process in any way, and I will see to it that you don't design anything more exciting than a garage for the rest of your mediocre career in this city!"

"And I'll warn you, Thad. Buck the wishes of your own family and your Plan will be doomed."

"In view of your position, which is weak indeed, I'd say your threats are rather empty. Besides," Thaddeus gained sudden control. He would show this aging *enfant terrible* that he was dealing with someone who knew all of the strengths and weaknesses of the game, "if you really care about Jane . . . and *her* daughter . . . you'll not oppose the Plan as drawn."

Peter O'Malley was silenced. The intercom broke the quiet.

"Mr. Ash, is your brother's current address still in Denver?" The sweetness of Miss Pierce's inquiry increased Thaddeus's resolve to relieve her. She was well aware that Thaddeus wasn't alone. Subterfuge. Everywhere subterfuge.

Thaddeus slammed his palm down on the intercom. "Yes, Denver. Now, I'm still in conference. Please don't disturb us again."

"Yes, sir." Thaddeus thought he detected the flavor of sarcasm about her words. Perhaps she was one of O'Malley's zany minority as well.

"Your brother?" O'Malley's lips formed a half smile.

"That's none of your business."

"Whether it is or not, the rumors must be true."

"I don't know what you mean, and I don't care to." Of course, Thaddeus did want to know exactly what O'Malley meant. Peter promptly obliged him.

"So Jane was right. It's not all neatly signed and sealed."

"I'm late for my next appointment—my next *scheduled* appointment."

"We'll have another opportunity, Thad."

"I doubt it. Now, good afternoon."

They neither shook hands nor expressed any final niceties. O'Malley turned and left. Thaddeus seethed, staring out his window towards the West, wondering whether he would ever be truly free from a family into which he wished he had never been born.

CHAPTER 3

Down from the Mountain

JAMES WHITTLESWORTH ASH, uncle and great-uncle to nieces and nephews he had never seen nor even knew existed, rose from his simple bed of box springs, mattress, and covers, stood before the smoky glass of his fiftieth-floor bedroom, and sighed. It was the nineteenth of December—a year to the day from when his brother John had died.

The Christmas season had been allowed to pass by, year after year, without notice since Whittlesworth was twenty. It had never bothered him before.

Not that Whittlesworth was stingy or miserly or mean-hearted. He gave to many approved charities—though with the exception of one he never participated in their selection. That was always done from a distance, by a committee or a trusted employee or, on occasion, at random. He would give to the Red Cross one year, the March of Dimes the next, an obscure college still another.

Nor was Whittlesworth cruel or spiteful. He had never committed a purposefully malicious act. Yet there existed in his life a gaping void where emotion and caring and the need for humanity should have resided. It had once been there, but it had been stolen at some point. Like a homeowner violated by the theft of his personal

27

goods, Whittlesworth had never recovered from the sense of loss. It had nagged at him and gotten worse, until his feelings of violation were the empty replacement for the emotions that were absent. As for Christmas, it had been relegated to a day and a season to be practiced by relatives far away in time and space. That's the way it had been for some fifty-five years.

There had been times in the dark of the night, after the years of buying and selling were done and that responsibility was delegated to a board of directors, that Whittlesworth had longed for his brother John—the little boy who had always tagged along to the creeks and the fields nestled within their city's immense central park. The little boy who had looked to his older brother for guidance on such topics as Santa Claus and God and girls. The little boy who had gloried in the presence of his older brother. Whittlesworth was only a few years older, but to John he had been a protector, a confessor, and always a hero of Promethian proportions.

Whittlesworth had longed for John the young man as well—the young man who had shared his dreams of a limitless future. The young man who had offered consolation and understanding when their father had borne down harder and more harshly, always trying to mold Whittlesworth, the dreamer and poet, into his own ideal of greatness. Years later Whittlesworth would exceed even his father's ideal, but in the process the dreamer and poet would be subverted.

Whittlesworth had shared more than dreams with John. On the night he left he had made it very clear. "She likes us both, little brother," he had said. "I'm dropping out of the race. I can't stay here anymore. If you win her heart, then good for you." They had grasped hands—a pact of sorts—then embraced. A freight train had carried him westward. All so many years before.

Then John died, breaking Whittlesworth's last blood link with a past that he had at times scorned and at other times ignored. There were other relatives—even a brother whom he had never met. A late-life replacement, perhaps, for the failure which Whittlesworth had become in his father's eyes. But Whittlesworth felt no affinity for Thaddeus. He was just another man with whom he shared a surname.

There was Helen, the girl whose favor he had yielded to John more than half a century before. The girl who had stirred both the dreamer and the poet in him. But she had long since become an element in John's life, not his. John was the last one who could have reforged Whittlesworth's ties with the past. And John was dead.

Now Whittlesworth was dying. Doctors had diagnosed the weakening of his heart muscles nearly two years before. When they had prescribed the laundry list of medications, they had told him his condition would progressively worsen. Nothing he could do would change that. No amount of exercise or diet or surgery.

Whittlesworth had laughed at the irony of their observation that he just couldn't have a new heart. They had no idea who he was; he had secured his anonymity even with them. He could have bought entire hospitals. Dozens of donor hearts were available to him. But age had finally trapped him; he was too old and weak to survive the operation. And not just one physician told him. Whole teams of them said it. So he took pills and waited, a semi-invalid, for the end to come at some ill-defined moment in the future.

Whittlesworth took a breath—as deeply as he could—and slipped on his old velvet smoking jacket. He walked to the Victorian secretary in the corner of the starkly painted room—the one inheritance of his father that he had accepted thirty years before, and a twin to the one which remained at the mansion—and read again the two letters before him. The first was written in the hand of a child—a little girl who claimed to be his great niece—and the second was a puffed-up piece of fluff from his youngest brother. He shuffled to his closet, where he placed them inside of an old blue suit.

Whittlesworth was going home. Too late perhaps, but he would undertake the venture all the same. Two days before, after he had mulled over the letters again and again, the decision had suddenly occurred to him in the middle of the night. He had awakened as fresh as if he had been sleeping forever. It was three in the morning. He was going home. That was a certainty. And as certain as he was that he would go, he was just as uncertain why. That part had puzzled him these past forty-eight hours. Why? What a simple question to find so complex and confounding. Perhaps the answer would come with the effort.

Like a young boy packing for his first summer at camp, Whittlesworth had prepared both the tangible and intangible wealth of his life for whatever lay ahead. One antiquated leather suitcase bore all of the clothes he thought he would need. Another bag—an old black leather satchel—held nearly half a million dollars in various denominations. It was the same black satchel that had belonged to his grandfather and which he had taken on the boxcar west the night he had left home. Back then it held a change of clothes, a toothbrush, and four dollars.

The less liquid possessions which marked the all-too-generous estate of James Whittlesworth Ash were safely in trust, neatly spelled out on his attorney's letterhead and tucked into the inner pocket of the satchel. It was even signed. He needed only to type in the names of the beneficiaries. It might be the family he had never seen or, if they didn't strike his fancy, the mailman. It was nice to leave a part of the future uncertain.

Fairly neat way of wrapping things up, he thought, even if it had taken a small team of lawyers all day to come up with it. They had earned their pay. All that remained were the corporate assets, and as far as he was concerned, the corporate shareholders were welcome to the profits. Everything had been quite simple—except the business about the property back home. At first he had been tempted to simply sign Thaddeus's power of attorney. No muss, no fuss. What did he care? But when he had asked himself that question, the answer had been anything but clear and forthcoming. Then had come the waking in the night.

Whittlesworth set both of his bags by the door of his apartment, then paused to catch his breath. Even a few steps wore him out. He returned to the secretary and examined the letter he had finished the night before—a "farewell, thanks, don't follow me" note to a lieutenant whom he trusted more than any human being on the face of the earth, and had never seen. Maybe he was as eccentric as the gossip columnists made him out to be. What did he care? They hadn't been with him during the lean years and certainly had no hand in creating the fat years. So why not feed the flames of their imaginations during his sunset years? If they only knew. They'd have a field day wondering where he had gone and to whom he would leave his fortune. They had already had a field day wondering about his health.

Whittlesworth chuckled as he recalled the garage attendant's astonishment when he had informed him that it was finally time to tune up the old '56 Cadillac and put some new tires on it. "Have it ready in a day—and not a word to anyone. There's a hundred-dollar tip in it," he had told the man. Silence had been assured at least a dozen times. Like the doctors, the garage attendant had no idea just whose tip he was hustling.

Whittlesworth hadn't driven an automobile in twenty-five years. Any difficulties along the way could be fatal, but he had long since ceased to care about his ultimate end. It would come when it would come. Like an animal returning to its birthplace, James Whittlesworth Ash was blinded from danger by a compulsion to close the circle of his life.

Now it was all in place. The sun was rising in the east and he was ready for it. He undressed deliberately, then put on a fresh shirt and his wool suit pants. A thrill ran through him as he put on his coat, his overcoat, then his hat, and looked around his pristine living quarters one last time. He rather liked the idea of running away from home again as he had more than a half century before.

He closed the door and left by the private elevator he had had installed when he had built his tower almost thirty years before. It hadn't seen much use, other than carrying breakfast, dinner, mail, and, more recently, himself on his secretive trips to the doctors'. No one was up and around, and no one was present to question him as he climbed into his Cadillac. The old engine purred contentedly. The mechanics had done a good job. He heaved his bags into the back seat and put his maps by his side. He wondered for a moment how differently the countryside might look this time around. Then he pressed his foot on the accelerator, left the garage, turned to the east, and drove out of town. Still thinking of both Katie's and Thaddeus's letters, Whittlesworth drove all day and into the night, ignoring the clouds which gathered to the north of him, thick with snow.

CHAPTER 4

Dub and Buddy

PIERCING BRIGHT LIGHTS seemed suddenly to bear down on them. Alarms were going off like a series of explosions. The taller man grabbed his companion.

"Buddy . . . leave the junk . . . we'll come back!"

Buddy obeyed, dropping the aluminum cans he had been fishing out of the dumpster at the rear of the store. As he did, he heard Dub's voice again, this time in a hushed whisper.

"Look. By the building over there."

Buddy twisted his head to the left and squinted. Two teenagers were running down the side of the building, legs pounding, their arms filled with stolen stereo equipment. They were running for the back alley, directly towards Dub and Buddy. The sound of police sirens now compounded the whine of the private alarm which the young burglars had set off. They had shattered Dub and Buddy's sojourn through the fresh garbage and aluminum scrap placed for pick-up the next morning, and Dub was in no mood to forgive and forget.

"Damn it," he growled. "Those jerks just knocked off that store there, and the cops'll think it was us."

"Yeah . . . let's run." Buddy was already searching the alley for a hiding place—some dark hole into which he could desperately crawl before the inevitable arrest and the fruitless attempt to explain why he and Dub had been back there. The sound of the police siren was coming nearer by the second. Headlights suddenly turned the corner of the alley some fifty yards away.

"I'm not getting hauled in for these losers." Dub pointed to the two young men almost upon them. Dub was tough for an old guy. That's why Buddy loved him. "Here, grab this garbage can." Buddy did as he was told. He had always done as Dub told him. Dub was in charge. Always. "Now, quick . . . here they come. Do what I do."

Buddy obediently watched as Dub flung a garbage can from the shadows of the dumpster into the path of the first running figure. Buddy did the same to the second. The two went down in the middle of the alley, sprawling amidst the collection of commercial and residential refuse—packing cardboard and milk jugs, computer paper and coffee grounds. The police cruiser's brakes squealed, the car stopping just short of where the two slipped and fell in the trap thrown at them by Dub and Buddy.

"Come on, Dub!" Buddy wasn't supposed to think for them. Dub was the planner, but Buddy was scared—too scared to wait for Dub's order. He darted from the friendly shadows of the dumpster and started down the middle of the alley like a frightened deer. Dub had no choice but to follow. He couldn't let Buddy get caught and maybe arrested just for being at the wrong place at the wrong time. Hell, they had just performed a public service! Dub yelled at the young cop who had started for Buddy, then ran as fast as he could on legs which had seen over seventy winters drift by aimlessly, one into another.

"Stop! You're both under arrest!" Dub turned briefly. The police spotlight caught him directly in the eyes. "You . . . old man . . . stop! You are under arrest!" Dub had done the one thing he had learned years ago never to do. He had turned his face into their light. You never did that and survived very long on the road or in the city streets. Dub was into the next block, a block of houses now, and he saw a side yard where there were no prohibiting fences or gates. Dropping his right shoulder, he veered into the back yard of the house, feet scrabbling for traction on the frozen ground. He was nearly to the front of the house when the young cop's bobbing flashlight beam caught him.

"Get back here, Harter. These are the guys we want." Dub could hear the faint growl of an older voice a block away. "Leave the winos alone. They aren't worth anything."

The young cop's flashlight switched off. Dub was safe. He slowed down, his breath coming in desperate gasps. Damned cops had a lot of nerve. "Winos." "Not worth anything." He had broken guys' noses and kicked out their teeth for less than that.

"Dub . . . hey, Dub—over here."

"Buddy . . . where are you?" Dub stared in the direction of Buddy's voice, peering into the darkness until Buddy scrambled from beneath the safety of a bush.

"I'm okay," Buddy whispered. "Let's get out of here."

"Did you hear what that old cop said?" Dub's voice was louder, belligerent.

"Forget it, Dub."

"Forget, hell. I'm going back. I swear I'm going back."

Buddy knew his friend all too well. He would posture and jut out his jaw and gesture with his fist, just like he had in the old days when he had been a drinking man. Dub hadn't been drinking for almost ten years. It had something to do with what a doctor down South had told him. Not that Dub had ever been a steady patron of the grape. But in his day he had enjoyed a nip. When he was good and tanked, this was how he sounded. And when he sounded like this, Buddy had a routine that was pure vaudeville.

"Come on, Dub," he urged. "You don't want to hurt somebody." Buddy threw himself in front of his friend and leaned into his chest. "You'll hurt somebody, Dub. You don't wanna hurt somebody. Get all the cops lookin' for you for beating up a couple of 'em. You don't want that, huh? That ain't what you want, is it, Dub? Huh? Dub?"

Dub took a few steps forward, pushing Buddy with his chest, then relaxed. "No . . . no . . . I guess not . . . no." Dub was pleased. Once more his self-image had been affirmed, his manhood preserved.

Dub looked up at the old mansion whose side yard had provided their escape. It was dark except for a single light on the first floor and two on the second. Something about the place pleased him. Maybe it was the moment's euphoria. But there seemed to be more. Something beckoned, reminding him of a time long ago, when his mother and father and he had lived in a home sort of like this one. Long ago, before the Depression had wiped them out. Before his mother and father had died, consigning him to an aunt in the country with too many other mouths to feed. It wasn't the same house. It wasn't even the same city. But it was the same kind of house. Big and grand and imposing.

During their adventure their blood had run hot and they had both broken a sweat. Now, as their breathing calmed, they remembered with the first frigid breeze that it was below freezing.

"Where do you want to go tonight, Buddy?"

"Huh? Well, the Mission, I guess. What do you mean?"

"It'd be nice to sleep in a place like that, wouldn't it?" Dub nodded toward the old home. "With beds and hot showers and maybe a fireplace?"

"You been drinking, Dub?"

"Nah . . . just thinking."

"Let's get going."

"Okay." Dub yielded to Buddy's gentle tug and together they walked back towards the downtown, staying in the shadows of the old trees that lined the boulevard leading to the heart of the city. Instinctively they were still avoiding the police, though for what reason only their imaginations could answer. They walked for a mile or more until they came to the lighted cross of the Wayside Mission. Buddy smiled and rubbed his hands. Maybe the Mission would serve popcorn tonight. The soup kitchens always served popcorn near Christmas. Buddy started for the front door.

"Wait a minute." Dub held out his hand and stopped Buddy. Then he pointed to a bonfire set within an oil drum on a lot near the Mission. "Let's go over and warm ourselves for a second."

"But Dub, it's plenty warm inside."

"Suit yourself." Dub veered away from the Mission and strolled to the circle of shabby men huddled around the fire. Buddy hesitated for an instant, then followed. He always followed Dub.

Dub moved easily into the circle. It parted silently for Dub and Buddy while the man with the beard continued his harangue.

"I tell you, it ain't right. All around us . . . " the man swept his arm about in silence, "all around us. We beg . . . and they got it all." The man started weeping in his drunkenness. Several of the others started up the refrain, occasionally slipping a pint bottle from under their coats.

"Just told you . . . just told you . . . " the bearded man continued to no one in particular. "My little darling . . . my little darling. . . " His sentences and thoughts had been complete somewhere in his past; his present was a mere string of disjointed fragments.

"Listen." Dub's single, spoken word was a command. They all looked up and listened, straining to hear whatever the old man was talking about. "What do you hear?" No one answered. They were trying to hear something, anything. "That's life you're listening to," Dub told them. "The crackle of wood in a hot fire. The bellow of a barge down on the river. The sound of your own breathing. It's a song you guys are hearing. Only you don't know the words anymore." He fell silent, apparently unwilling to say more.

Dub was really feeling the evening. Buddy could tell. He had heard these thoughts before, expressed in years riding the rails and on migrant farms and along lonely stretches of highway. Dub was in his element.

"Tell 'em what they'd hear if they knew the words, Dub." Buddy liked this part. He knew that Dub liked it, too.

"Nah! You've heard it before . . . "

"Yeah, but I want to hear it again."

The scrap wood shifted in the barrel, and what seemed like a thousand red sparks whirled upwards, mixing with the large, wet flakes of snow that had begun to fall. Dub had their attention. Like an ancient shaman or a modern-day evangelist, he owned the audience.

"Well, okay then. You guys have forgotten how the tune goes and how the words sound. You used to know." There were a few nods and grumbles of assent. "You used to follow right along. Sometimes you did a little number all on your own. Sometimes you sang a solo. Other times you were just part of the chorus. But when the band played, you were right in step. Then something happened." More nods, more grumbles. "It didn't make any sense anymore. The noise was still there, but that was all it was—just noise. No tune that you could follow. No words that you could sing along with."

"So?" A short, mean-faced man stared at Dub across the flames belching up from the oil barrel.

"So we need to start our own tune. Any tune will do. The simpler, the better. As long as we create it, and learn it, and all share it, we'll be okay. As long as it's our tune . . . "

The sound of a car crashing into something forced them all to turn around. It was an old car, something from the fifties, and its headlights were skewed upwards at an angle, its left front tire resting on the curb. Dub's eyes narrowed with the fear they had all felt a thousand times before. At first he thought it might be the police back again. Then the door flew open, and an old man stumbled out. He stood up, trying to keep his balance as he moved towards them, hands outstretched. He weaved back and forth as if sobriety were a distant memory. Something about him frightened them. The out-of-place look of his clothes, the bulging-eyed expression which he had fixed in their direction, the odd manner in which his mouth kept opening and closing as if performing some bizarre pantomime.

"Help . . . help me . . . " The words finally emitted from the old man's open mouth like puffs of smoke. While the others backed farther away, Dub, and then Buddy, rushed towards him. The fellow stumbled, and Dub held out his arms. The old guy felt as light as a feather. It was hard to believe there was really a person under that big old overcoat of his. With one collapsing motion, the old man's body seemed to cave inward as it fell. Dub dropped to one knee. The stranger looked up and riveted his own eyes on Dub's. A look more of surprise than terror was highlighted by his open eyes and raised brows.

'Help me . . . " he repeated.

"What's hurting you, bud?" Dub wanted to help but he was powerless. The fellow was dying right before his eyes, and all he could do was try to comfort him.

"Help me . . . home . . . "

Dub smiled grimly. "That's everyone's problem here, pal."

"Take me . . . home . . . "

"Okay, we'll take you home, old timer." Fine thing calling him "old timer," Dub thought. He was probably about his own age. Dub turned to Buddy, who was hovering within inches of his shoulder. He shrugged slightly. They had been through similar scenes on more than one occasion.

The dying man grew desperate, grabbing Dub by the edges of his tattered overcoat. His strength took Dub by surprise. He started to jerk the man's clawing fingers away, then thought twice about it, and held them instead.

"Okay, okay. We'll get you home," Dub muttered.

"Too late," the old man hissed. "You . . . " he nodded to Dub, ". . . go home. Be . . . home . . . " It wasn't what the dying man had wanted to say, but his last ounce of adrenaline had played out.

"Is he dead, Dub?" Buddy's voice was tinged with fear—the fear of always being blamed for whatever happened.

Dub's voice was a solemn whisper. "Yeah, he's dead. The old guy never made it . . . " Dub lowered his body onto the cold ground. It remained obscured by the shadows from the sight of anyone on the street. Dub stood up slowly as if suddenly uncertain of where he was and what he was supposed to be doing.

"What do we do?" Buddy was on the verge of panic. He had lived through a score of deaths before, but he never knew how to handle its communication to the world at large.

"What? Oh . . . well, he looks like his clothes are worth something. We'll . . . um . . . have a look at the car in a minute. Cut the cards?" Dub graciously offered the corpse's possessions to the highest draw.

"Sure," Buddy stated hesitantly. He withdrew a grease-stained pack of cards from his pocket and cut them. He held a card to the light. Jack of Diamonds. Dub started to draw.

"No, listen . . . you can have 'em. I don't need 'em. You go ahead." Buddy's voice quavered. Dub held his card up anyway. It was the

King of Hearts. He returned the cards to Buddy and began to look through the dead man's clothes.

"You shouldn't do that, Dub," Buddy cautioned.

"I want to see what I've . . . what we've got here."

"If you're smart, we won't get anything. This guy's had a heart attack. Right now they won't do anything to us. You go to stealing his belongings, and we'll be in a helluva fix."

While Buddy rambled on, Dub searched the dead man's coat pockets. On one side he found a wallet containing no pictures, a long-expired driver's license, which he threw away, and hundreds of dollars. He couldn't believe it, but he retained his poker face throughout. On the other side there were two letters—one business, and one that looked like it was written by a little kid.

"We're going to be okay, Buddy. Here, help me get him over into those boxes." Buddy looked back first to see if they were being watched. The winos had scattered with the scent of impending death.

"Okay." Buddy grabbed the dead man's legs and carried him to the boxes, Dub clasping onto the corpse's shoulders. With quickness belying his seventy-plus years, Dub stripped him and exchanged clothes. Considering the man had weighed thirty pounds less than him, the clothes were a near perfect fit.

"Dub, you're going to stand out like a sore thumb. Take his wallet, change those clothes again, and let's get out of here."

"Shhh! Easy, Buddy."

"Don't mess with him, Dub. It's trouble."

"I won't get in any trouble. We'll see about the car in a minute. I won't take any chances."

"You're taking a chance right now!"

"Shhh!" Dub was holding the letters, first one, then the other, to the light while Buddy fussed and worried.

"What do those say?"

"Nothing."

"We're gettin' real secretive all of a sudden!"

"They say he's some guy from out of town . . . Colorado."

"And where are the letters from, Dub?"

"Here in town."

"Then he's somebody's grandpa home for Christmas! For Christ's sake, Dub, get out of those clothes. You give me the creeps."

"Nobody's going to catch me, or arrest me, or whatever. I think . . . maybe I'll just explore a little until I get tired of it. Then I'll come back, Buddy. Soon."

"Last time you said that, you were gone for three years."

"I came back, didn't I?" Buddy couldn't rebut Dub's irrefutable statement.

"Well, yeah," Buddy knew better than to argue with Dub when he got that screwy look in his eye, "but what do I do with this stiff dressed up like you?"

Dub smiled. "I always wanted to come to my own funeral. Kind of like Tom Sawyer, you know? Shame about crazy old Dub, eh?"

"I can't do that!"

"Sure you can. Who's gonna miss me? Seriously. Nobody except you. So just tell 'em I got too old, and the winter got too cold, and I just checked out. Bad ticker, you know." Dub nodded to his newly appointed deceased self. "He wasn't anybody to worry about. Old Dub just won't make the trip south this winter."

Though he wasn't drunk, big, drunken tears welled up in Buddy's eyes. "I don't think you'll be back soon, Dub. I don't think you'll be back ever." Dub and Buddy embraced, looking furtively around to make sure no one had seen their show of emotion.

"Buddy, my friend, I have enjoyed the company of your fire many times. If I need you, I'll call you here at the Mission and leave a message. But otherwise . . . have a Merry Christmas . . . I'll miss you . . . but this one I need to play alone for a while."

"All right." Buddy understood Dub's moods perfectly, even if at times he didn't understand their owner.

"Now, goodnight." Dub tipped the rim of the old fedora he had taken from James Whittlesworth Ash and retreated to the car, two leather bags, and a venture into chaos.

CHAPTER 5

Peter and Jane

JANE'S MORNING HAIR tumbled about her like Medusa's as she slumped back into the worn, velvet cushions of the kitchen's old oak chair. It was 9:00 A.M.—too early to be up and about during the holidays. Too early to have visitors. Certainly too early to be engaged in the absurd exercise of discussing life with Peter O'Malley. The steam from her double-scoop black coffee intermingled with blue tobacco smoke as Jane contemplated Peter's slightly graying mane. He was back, just as she was back, just as they had both sworn they would never be back again. Picking at each other. Playing their once-tried emotions all over again.

"Why don't *you* just go away for awhile." Jane hardly believed her own nerve. She took a long drag from her cigarette and looked away. The drawn tendons in her neck stood out like steel rods emerging from the collar of her flannel nightshirt. She couldn't stand looking at him when he was this way. She never could.

"You don't mean that." Peter smiled solicitously.

"Try me."

"You're smoking too much."

"That's my business."

"And Katie's."

41

Jane turned, her jaw set. She brought the cigarette to her lips and drew in on it defiantly.

"You're one to talk about Katie's welfare."

"Don't start that again. It wasn't that simple. You played your part. And I've done what we agreed."

"I know," was all that she said. It was all that she could say. Peter was right. She hated the martyrs in her sisterhood. She had no desire to join them. But that acknowledgment hardly resolved Peter's reoccurrence in her life.

"I should never have come back." She said it matter-of-factly, but it was meant as a confession of her own frailties.

"Sure you should have. This is home."

"I had a home in Boston."

"And a job which your paper terminated after the strike. No job, no rent, no home." Peter stood up and helped himself to another cup of coffee.

"I should've gone somewhere else."

"Wrong. Your mother couldn't have stayed here alone after your father died."

Jane sipped her own coffee. Peter was right again, but she wouldn't admit that twice in one morning, even to herself. She brushed the thought aside.

"Maybe."

"You know I'm right. Besides, you weren't about to just sit by and let Thaddeus bulldoze your home and ruin your neighborhood."

Jane smiled and shook her head. Salt and pepper brunette locks spewed right and left. The more she and Peter changed, the more they stayed the same.

"That is where you are definitely wrong. You're still living in another age. Wake up. The eighties just happened, not the sixties. I may give Thad a lot of crap, but in the end maybe he's right."

"You can't mean that."

"I can, and I do. If Thad's Plan can take care of Mother and Katie, and even me if I need it, what's more important, people or buildings?"

"But that's not the point!" Peter had begun to redden. Even his beard seemed to glow. She had always been able to raise the Irish in him. Jane gazed at him and smiled. He reminded her of a somewhat leaner, longer-haired architect with whom she had been infatuated and briefly married a thousand years before.

"Isn't it?"

"The point, Jane, is that you can have them both. And you can do better by the city and the people in the process!"

Jane held up her hand, her cigarette trailing smoke like a sky writer. "Save it for the rallies and the demonstrations."

"I won't go that far. I will, however, go to the board meeting
today."

"Big impression *you'll* make there."

"I can at least try. *I* still try, Jane."

Jane's eyes locked with his. Familiar feelings recurred—the sensa-
tion of tasting rich candy, of her heart seemingly lodged within her
throat. The irresistible desire to lock her body within his arms, to
grasp at his lips with hers. It was there. All there, buried beneath
mud-like layers of regret and betrayal. She forced herself to look
down at the table just as the phone rang. Damned phones, Jane
thought. Someday she would have to cut the wires and enjoy the
peace and quiet. It rang again.

"I've got it," Jane called out towards the upstairs. Her voice was
husky from the morning, her cigarette, and her last volley of feelings.

Jane picked up the receiver. "Hello." Jane could hear her mother's
voice on the upstairs phone. Thaddeus's flustered voice was already
in a state of high agitation.

"Has he been there?"

"Who?" Helen answered first.

"Whittlesworth, of course." Jane could hear and feel her mother's
breath robbed for an instant.

"What are you talking about, Thad?" Jane interceded.

"What do you mean, what am I talking about?"

"Don't get nasty."

"I needed his proxy. I hadn't heard from him. So I called out there
this morning and got his damned right-hand man out of bed. The old
man's flown the coop!"

"My, aren't we the warm and caring brother," Jane noted flatly.

"I care about the Plan, damn it!"

"Yes, Jane, dear. First things first." Helen's voice was pregnant
with sarcasm. "Brother be damned, save the Plan!"

Jane and Helen snickered quietly at Thaddeus's discomfort. Thaddeus started to respond, then paused. His brother? Even when he had
composed the letter—the very letter he was sure had won Whittlesworth's return—Thaddeus had not truly thought of Whittlesworth as a brother. The concept was foreign to him. One lunatic
brother was more than enough.

"Look, you two, I've heard he's sick. Or even dying. Maybe he's
senile!"

"Always hope for the best, Thad," Helen noted simply. He ignored
her as he always had.

"I'm going to call the police and tell them to keep a lookout."

"Very good, Thad. Arrest your brother when he gets to town."
Helen was in rare form. Jane started laughing out loud.

"Welcome home, Uncle Whittlesworth," Jane's voice dropped in
mock pontification. "Here's your padded cell! You are a warm one,
Uncle Thaddeus."

Jane switched the phone from one ear to the other and performed a
pirouette, the phone cord wrapping around her waist. Peter sensed
her whimsical mood, stood up, and started to untangle the cord. Jane
backed away. Conversation was one thing, physical contact was another. Katie appeared, all eyes and ears, at the door.

"Is Uncle Whittlesworth coming?" she whispered. Jane nodded
vigorously, then held her finger to her lips to gain Katie's silence.

"It's clear that I can't talk to you two! Just keep a lookout for him.
Call me if you hear anything." Thaddeus hung up without saying
good-bye.

"When?" Katie asked simply.

"We don't know . . . but Thaddeus seems to think he's coming."

"I knew it!" Peter clapped his hands together. "I knew it. There's
still a chance."

"I wouldn't make book on it just yet," Jane added.

"I knew he'd come." Katie started to brag about her letter, but
thought twice and merely repeated herself. "I knew he'd come."

"That's right, darling. Now, hurry upstairs and help mother make
the beds and straighten up the bathroom."

"Yes, Katie, er . . . do what your mom says." Peter forever found
himself tongue-tied in Katie's presence. She was still so new to him,
so wondrous and mysterious—separate, yet a part of him. She was
like a Christmas present left by Santa Claus, perfect in its presenta-
tion, but untouchable. Katie turned and raced from the kitchen up
the back stairs.

"Jane." Peter's voice was thick and uncertain, "I really think we
should . . . I mean, we need to . . . "

"You do, and I'll never talk to you again. We're friends. I can live
with that. Katie can live with that. Katie's father is dead. Remember
that."

"If we were really stuck with that story, I couldn't have come over
this morning."

"You're here, in this kitchen, because I let you in the door. I can
also show you out the door. That was resolved a long time ago."

"Now you're thinking of yourself and your own pride, and . . . "
The phone rang again before Peter could struggle through the rest of
his thought.

"Hello!" Jane had grabbed the receiver all too eagerly. Past thoughts of the evils of the telephone were instantly erased.

"Is this the Ash residence?" The voice was polite, official sounding.

"Yes, it is."

"Okay. Well, this is Sergeant Banta, with the city police."

"Is something wrong?" Jane interrupted. Peter heard the concern in her voice.

"What is it?" he said. Jane shook her head to gain his silence and to listen more closely.

"No cause for alarm. We've got a relative of yours down here at the second district station. He's a little confused, but I think his name is James W. Ash. Is that, uh . . . "

"My great uncle!" Jane's words had almost stuck in her throat.

"Is it Uncle Whittlesworth?" Peter's voice was as frantic as Jane's was muffled. Jane nodded weakly.

"So, you want us to hold him here until you all can come down to get him?" Jane held her hand over the mouthpiece.

"Peter, they want us to pick him up down at the second district." Her voice was dreamlike and distant.

"Tell him I'm on my way!" Peter was halfway out the door before Jane could reformulate Peter's message to the officer on the other end of the line.

CHAPTER 6

The Interrogation

"Now, let's have it one more time. Where did you say you were coming from, and who did you say you were going to see." Sergeant Harter put out his cigarette and took one last gulp of cold coffee. Youth and total lack of seniority had entrapped him in a twelve-hour shift in the early morning hours two days before Christmas. The night before he had been riding shotgun in a patrol car; now he was processing the dawn patrol—drunks, derelicts, and ding-a-lings. Merry Christmas.

Whittlesworth had recognized Sergeant Harter immediately. He was only astounded that Harter had not recognized him. Clothes must indeed make—or remake—the man. "Now, let me think for a moment," he said deliberately, having dodged the question twice before. He rolled his eyes upwards, absorbing every greasy spot on the room's industrial yellow-painted concrete blocks. Better they think he was crazy than lying. If he could just get out the door, he'd be back with Buddy heading for a southbound freight in an hour. What had he been thinking? Why had he hung around this town? First things first. Try to remember the postmark on that letter.

"I think I got something here." Sergeant Banta stuck his head in from the office next door, the white pages of

47

the phone book open before him. Sergeant Harter turned to his fellow public servant, and when he did, Whittlesworth quickly withdrew the letters from his pocket, glanced at the postmark and address, then slipped them back in. Harter turned around. Whittlesworth smiled serenely at him and picked up his statement in mid-stride, ". . . yes, that's it, I was driving in from Denver to see my brother, Thaddeus, and my great niece, Katie. And so, if you don't mind, I'll be going. . . ." Whittlesworth stood up and Sergeant Harter placed his palm lightly on Whittlesworth's shoulder. Something bothered him about this fellow. Something wasn't right. In his slumber-starved mind a synapse had widened, precluding him from a thought that yearned for completion.

"Not so fast, old fellow. Have we met somewhere before? I mean, did you *just* get in from Denver, or have you been in town for awhile?"

"Well, I don't think we've met . . . no . . . can't say that. And I didn't *just* get in town from Denver. Can't say that, either. No, I was just driving through town when that snowball hit my window . . . "

"Yeah, right in front of the mayor's house."

"I assure you I didn't know whose house it was—or whose snowball."

"So what made you attack the mayor's kids, anyway?"

Whittlesworth took a deep breath and tried to answer the question for himself before he tried answering it for the sergeant. Less than eight hours before he had sworn to Buddy that he'd be careful. He had sworn to himself that he was just taking the clothes and the wallet full of money and the car for a lark. He would dump the car later, when it ran out of gas.

Then he had checked into that motel for the night and opened the black satchel. Where had all that money come from? And where was the old man taking it? And what was *he* doing sticking around town with all that dough? It didn't make any sense, but somehow it seemed right. Just like it seemed right to keep the car and fill it up with gas. Just like it seemed right to stop for breakfast and sit at the counter for anyone to see. Just like it seemed right—and natural as could be—to revert to his childhood when that fat, soggy snowball had splattered on the windshield before his eyes.

"I didn't attack them," Whittlesworth said very seriously. "They attacked me."

"Those kids are five, seven, eight, and eleven, buddy. What do you mean, they *attacked* you?"

"Well, not attacked exactly . . . but they challenged me. And, well," Whittlesworth gave the wide, innocent grin he had begun to affect, "I couldn't resist. They all looked so deserving in front of that white house with the columns across the front."

"Right . . . well, if the mayor decides to press charges . . . "

"Hey, Joe," the voice of Sergeant Banta came from the next room, "there's two Ash families here that might fit. There's a Thaddeus and a John."

"Yes, that's it!" Whittlesworth tried to rise again.

Harter's hand went out automatically. "Okay, okay—now, where do they live?" Whittlesworth had no idea that his immediate predecessor would have no idea where Thaddeus lived. He grasped for an answer and remembered Katie's letter. "Park Place . . . I can't remember the number, but . . . "

"That's it, all right." Sergeant Banta became his angel of salvation. "John W. Ash, 31 Park Place. That's the old Ash mansion."

"Hmmm." Sergeant Harter locked eyes with Whittlesworth. Neither blinked. Harter rubbed the back of his neck.

"You have anything to do with that new development plan they got going for that area of town?" Again the interrupting voice of Sergeant Banta.

"Indirectly," Whittlesworth ventured.

"Well, wait a minute," Banta called out. Sergeant Harter, handicapped by exhaustion, continued to examine Whittlesworth until his partner emerged from the next room. "Here it is. I knew I saw your name somewhere. Why didn't you tell us who you were? It was in the paper yesterday." The desk sergeant thrust a newspaper stained with coffee and corned beef into Whittlesworth's hands. Whittlesworth took it in like air. Eccentric millionaire . . . seldom if ever seen in public . . . rumored to be coming home. . . .

"Yes, that's me," Whittlesworth said. Relief washed over him, followed rapidly by the unsettling realization that he had just entrapped himself within the very persona Buddy had cautioned him to avoid.

"Okay." Sergeant Banta grinned. "You just make yourself at home, and I'll contact your family."

Whittlesworth tried to relax even as Sergeant Harter continued to circle the room like a lion sizing up its breakfast. Knowledge was a wonderful thing, Whittlesworth thought, except when it provided just enough information to confuse him more than ever before. So what was this recluse Whittlesworth? A nut? A developer?

What was he supposed to do now that they were calling "his" family on the phone? If he could only make it out the door alone. He couldn't carry off being someone he wasn't. Maybe to two policemen, but not to his family.

Ten minutes passed like one excruciating hour after another. Whittlesworth inspected every certificate, every citation for valor, every photo, and every framed letter on the walls. Under the watchful glances of Sergeant Harter, he took out and examined again and again the two letters from "his" relatives. Somehow he had to piece things together. Figure out how he would make it through the next few hours and then escape.

Escape. He wasn't a man who appreciated confinement. He had survived most of his life traveling from one seasonal job to the next, picking fruit, carnival work, running the rides for the state fairs, staking tobacco. Anything more than a few months in one location was tantamount to a jail sentence for this man who now found himself walled inside a respectable businessman's identity.

If they found the other body, and if they checked his face against this fellow driving in from Denver, then he'd be in real trouble. Sure, no one knew the homeless hobo named Dub. Unless it was Buddy, and Buddy would play it all pretty close. But what if someone at the Mission had remembered him from the one or two meals he and Buddy had taken there or the fireside speech? It wasn't likely, but it could happen. If there were any questions asked at all, he'd be the first one they would grill. Even if he told the truth, even if Buddy stood by every word, he'd be arrested and tried for something. He knew how the system worked. He couldn't afford a lawyer. The public defender's office might not have time for a case that insignificant for months or even years. And so he would sit in jail. And sitting in jail would be a sentence of death. Every day of freedom had become precious to him these last few years. Age had seemed to pass him by until just recently. Then it had captured him with a vengeance. With the change of every season, he actually felt older. Incarcerated, age would take still more from him every day. Incarcerated, he would die. It was all as clear as the citations for valor on the yellow block wall.

"Okay, Mr. Ash, there's someone here to see you," said Sergeant Banta. Whittlesworth's heart fluttered with the sudden rush of adrenaline, then started racing. This was it. The beginning of his inevitable demise. It was over. He deserved it. He had been stupid.

Peter O'Malley strode into the room with a big grin on his face. Whittlesworth's eyes grew large, his body stiff. He must not say anything. He must make this young man speak first. Was this his grandson? A nephew? Child of a friend. The possibilities were limitless.

"You must be Uncle Whittlesworth!" Why was this young man unsure?

"And you are?"

"I'm Peter O'Malley . . . um . . . a friend of your niece, Jane." Why had this fellow hesitated over his connection to the Ash family? Maybe he was uncertain about his identity, too.

"And you're here to pick me up?"

"Well, they said out at the front desk that the police have impounded your car. We can get it right after Christmas. The important thing now is that I get you home."

"Home . . . right."

"Do you feel all right?"

"I've felt better. Just a little tired. Long trip, you know."

"Right. I mean, you fooled everybody actually coming. Thaddeus was sure you'd just send your proxy." Proxy. What was a proxy? It had been mentioned in the letter. What was it for? Was he supposed to have it with him? Was it a thing or a person?

"No . . . I wouldn't send . . . it."

"That's what Katie's been saying." Whittlesworth noticed that the young man's voice dropped as he mentioned Katie's name. Who was he in relation to Katie?

"Yes, indeed. Katie. I'm . . . er . . . looking forward to meeting her."

"Okay. Well," Peter turned to the two sergeants who had been absorbing the prattle, "I guess we're ready to leave?"

"Absolutely. You can pick up your suitcases at the cage." Sergeant Banta beamed. "Sorry for the mix-up, Mr. Ash, sir."

"No problem, officer." Whittlesworth waved away his concern with a flick of his trembling fingers. "I started all the trouble. Just my eccentricity, I suppose, eh?"

"It'll come to me . . . " was all that Sergeant Harter said, forcing a half smile.

"Don't lose any sleep over it, officer." Whittlesworth gave a little half-hearted salute and departed the company of the local gendarmes.

CHAPTER 7

The Heavy Laden

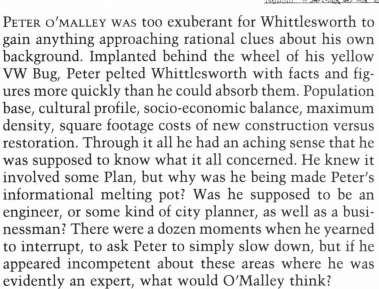

PETER O'MALLEY WAS too exuberant for Whittlesworth to gain anything approaching rational clues about his own background. Implanted behind the wheel of his yellow VW Bug, Peter pelted Whittlesworth with facts and figures more quickly than he could absorb them. Population base, cultural profile, socio-economic balance, maximum density, square footage costs of new construction versus restoration. Through it all he had an aching sense that he was supposed to know what it all concerned. He knew it involved some Plan, but why was he being made Peter's informational melting pot? Was he supposed to be an engineer, or some kind of city planner, as well as a businessman? There were a dozen moments when he yearned to interrupt, to ask Peter to simply slow down, but if he appeared incompetent about these areas where he was evidently an expert, what would O'Malley think?

"Just who are you again?" Whittlesworth finally interrupted out of sheer frustration.

"Me?" Peter responded like a deflating balloon. "To be honest about it, in the big scheme of things, I'm nobody."

"I don't get it. You're picking me up . . . on behalf of my family. And you know more about the Plan than any crew of men . . . but you're nobody? That doesn't square."

"Well . . . in the family, I'm Jane's friend. That's all. Not husband, nor fiancé, nor even lover. We were once—all three that is—but that was a long time ago."

"I see."

"And as far as the Plan, well, I'm sort of an interloper . . . a neighborhood activist. To Thad I'm a pain in the neck."

Whittlesworth looked around him. A city park was laid out along the road that could have been acreage lifted from virgin forest. He had seen woods like this in North Carolina, Indiana, Pennsylvania, Kentucky, and even Missouri—the last of the W.P.A. projects, national parks and national forests. Adjacent to the park were elegant, old, brick Victorian homes, topped with mansard roofs and rimmed with vestiges of rusted wrought-iron gates and fences. About it all there was more than a shading of shabbiness and even decay.

"This your neighborhood, Mr. Activist?"

"Yeah. Sort of. I live in an apartment over on the other end of the park. I grew up in the West End. My aunt lived in that place right there." Peter slowed down to point. "She was one of your teachers." The terror returned—the knowledge that one informant's quavering finger at the imposter would condemn him to unalterable discomfort.

"Don't bother stopping." Whittlesworth's voice cracked. "I wouldn't want to disturb her this early in the day."

Peter laughed softly. "She's gone now. Almost ten years. She hadn't lived there since I was a little boy."

"Yes, well, and her name was O'Malley?"

"Yes."

"Oh yes, I remember now. Fine teacher." Whittlesworth had to walk the razor's edge between the failure of his memory and its vividness.

"She always said you were one of her best students."

"Well, she flattered me." Whittlesworth glanced at Peter from the corner of his eye. "I always worked very hard, applied myself, studied late into the night . . . "

"That must have made a racket."

"Huh?"

"Playing the trumpet so late at night!"

"Oh, yes. Well, I had a very tolerant mother." Whittlesworth grew silent. Enough wing-spreading for awhile.

"Do you know where you are now?"

Whittlesworth felt like he was back in school. He hated tests then. He hated them more now. "I recognize my old city, Peter." Of course,

he didn't. "But a lot has changed in, well, a lot of years have gone by."
Dates, names, places, and events were to be avoided. Vague—he had
to be vague. Be vague long enough to make his escape. *How* had he let
himself get into this fix?

"Okay. Well, you recognize the mansion and Whittlesworth
Park?" Sweat broke out over the top of his lip. Whittlesworth stared
intently out the window at the homes passing by. "Yes, of course."
He looked back at Peter, trying to read the direction of the young
man's eyes. Peter nodded up to the right. Whittlesworth jerked back
around and was hit by a sudden sense of déjà vu. This old mansion
was familiar—its shape, its landscaping, the tall windows and doors.
He could see it all indistinctly in his memory, as in a dream. Maybe
the dead man's spirit was beginning to possess him. He definitely had
to get away as soon as possible. Forget the black leather bag in the
back seat of the VW; just get out and run. Then it came to him. He
wasn't crazy and he wasn't possessed. It was the house he had admired just the night before. He and Buddy had been there. They had
trod its grounds and hidden in its shadows.

"Look." Peter had finally stopped the car, holding it idling in the
middle of the boulevard. "I know I'm supposed to get you back home.
And I know everyone is expecting you. But how 'bout a drive around
the perimeter of the park? It's only a mile or two."

"Whatever you say." Why wasn't he making a break for it? This
could be his only chance.

"Great." Peter shifted into gear and pulled back into the right-hand
lane. "Did you ever know your Uncle James Whittlesworth?" Peter
asked.

"No," Whittlesworth murmured, assembling facts and making
guesses, "At least, not that I can recall."

"He had a lot of foresight to lay out this park in the middle of the
woods and farmland."

"Yes . . . indeed he did."

"My great grandfather, Robert O'Malley, drew up most of the
landscaping."

"Is that so," Whittlesworth mumbled, wishing Peter would watch
the road and not him.

"And he would tell me stories of how he worked with your uncle
on every detail, so that nature and man would exist in harmony."

"That so?" Whittlesworth began to admire the splendor of the area
around him. It *was* a nice park.

"It's all coming down," Peter said abruptly. "The new arena will
take out the park—along with parking, of course."

Whittlesworth suddenly understood that he was on a guided tour on behalf of the Plan's disloyal opposition. No wonder young O'Malley was on the outs with both the family and the Plan. He also understood that there was strength in numbers. As far as he could tell, Peter was a committee of one.

"You have a problem with progress, young man?"

"When it's progress, no. When it's a short-term advantage for the greedy, yes!"

"That's your opinion, isn't it?"

"Yes, I suppose it is."

"And you're alone in that opinion?"

"No. The people who still live here are with me. So are a few of the older merchants. And there's the . . . "

"But most of them don't own the property, do they?"

"You should know. Your father was the one who insisted the property would stay in the family. 'Lease, but never sell'—that was his motto."

"Ah, yes . . . lease. And, er, what about the leases?" Whittlesworth hoped that Peter would help him out.

"The last long-term lease ran out three years ago. That's when your brother started his little Plan."

"Yes. Very industrious. Very ambitious."

"Very . . . " Peter held his comment to himself. If he wanted to win Whittlesworth over, he would do better not to denigrate his youngest brother. "Very much unlike John. John was all for spending the money to bring this area back."

"But John's dead now."

"Yes. But his spirit lives."

"In you?"

"I'd like to think so." Peter grew silent. Whittlesworth's mystique had suddenly waned. He was just another developer—no magic, no whimsy, no romance. Like the others, he had made his money through the god of expediency. "Look," he finally said, "you remember St. Andrew's, don't you?" Whittlesworth sensed another trap.

"Yes, I suppose. It's been a long time . . . "

"Okay. Then stop with me for a second. I want you to meet someone. A friend of mine. I want you to see what he's struggling with at the church, then I'll get you back home."

"I don't know."

"Please." There was a longing in Peter's voice. It was the cry of the underdog which Whittlesworth had so often heard during a lifetime on the road. It was a cry that he was powerless to assuage. He was too old, too uncertain, too in need of simple escape from this predicament. But even as he thought these things, he realized that he couldn't turn down this young idealist's simple request. He couldn't help Peter, but he could avoid hurting him any further.

"Okay. But just a few minutes. Then I think I want to get back to this family I haven't seen . . . in a while." Whittlesworth surprised himself with the conviction that rang in his own quiet statement. Lord, was *he* beginning to believe his own lie?

They drove on in silence for a moment, then Peter pulled over to the curb in front of a stone church nestled between two nondescript commercial properties. Peter got out of the car and Whittlesworth followed his lead. They walked up the old brick walkway, through a high, iron gate, and into the side entrance. Whittlesworth wished they had gone around to the front entrance. He was sure that he was supposed to know this church and its history and, from their approach, it bore no hint of its identity or denomination. It looked Episcopalian, he thought, or Catholic, but he had no idea.

"The man I want to introduce you to knows you very well . . . *very* well!" Peter smiled. Whittlesworth suddenly balked. He was out of the car. Perhaps this was the time to run. He might never get another chance. Discovery was waiting in the church. He slowly backed away. Instead of proceeding without noticing, as Whittlesworth had hoped might be the case, Peter immediately came back for him.

"Don't get stage fright. I know you haven't been here for fifty years or so, but you're going to find some good memories within these walls."

"I'll be the judge of that."

Peter's smiled faded. "I'm sorry. I know you had some rough times way back then, but legend has it that some of your best moments were spent around St. Andrew's."

"Well, that was then, and this is now. I think we'd better go." Whittlesworth turned just as a voice called at them from the door.

"Peter. What are you doing out there? It's cold. Get in here right this minute!" Whittlesworth knew without looking that this was the man who knew him so well. His body chilled as he tried to raise his overcoat against the elements that were more within him than carried by the cold December air. His efforts failed. His teeth started chattering.

"Mr. Ash," Peter said, holding his arm, "you're shaking all over. I'm sorry. I wasn't thinking about the cold. Let's get you inside." Inside, Whittlesworth thought—the one place he didn't want to be. He was powerless to resist. Like the condemned being led to the scaffold, Whittlesworth shuffled weakly at Peter's side, the minister in the door looming ever larger. He was tall, dressed in a priest's garb, a black man with graying hair. Who was he in the life of Whittlesworth?

"James Whittlesworth Ash." The man spoke to him before he had reached the door. Whittlesworth tried to imagine how he could be this errant. He must be myopic. If he knew Whittlesworth, he certainly knew who wasn't walking forward hanging onto Peter O'Malley's arm.

"I'm sorry, it's been a long time," he croaked. "And I've changed a lot. Names lately escape me. You're going to have to excuse me . . . "

"Please. Please. No excuses." Easy for the cleric to say. How long before he would realize the truth? "You're absolutely innocent in this instance." Already he was receiving false pardon for the crime or crimes of which he was sure that he would be convicted. "We've never had the pleasure. I'm Jim Spencer, rector here at St. Andrew's." Never had the pleasure? Of what? Meeting? Peter had just assured him that Spencer knew him quite well.

"But, you know me?" Whittlesworth ventured hesitantly.

"Know *of you*, Mr. Ash. Know of your history in this church during your youth. Know of your anonymous generosity through the years. We weren't supposed to know, of course, but how many benefactors from Colorado would St. Andrew's have?" Spencer didn't know him. He knew of him. There was an immense difference. Whittlesworth took a deep breath and straightened his shoulders. If O'Malley did this to him again, he was going to slug him.

"Mr. Spencer, it's a great pleasure. It's, er, a bit of a shock that you've found me out. But that was . . . poor planning on my part."

James Spencer extended his hand and Whittlesworth took it. Spencer had a firm, dry grasp. Worn hands. Working hands. He liked this fellow; he seemed less like an executioner each moment. He liked his dignified demeanor, his soft Carolina accent, the way the right side of his mouth raised higher than the left when he grinned. He liked the sparkle of his eyes. Everything about him was natural and honest.

"I'm glad Peter has brought you by. Rumors were flying about whether you were coming back home or not, and I told Peter to drop by if the rumors proved true."

"Actually, Jim, I've just picked Mr. Ash up from . . . well, he had car trouble, and I'm giving him a ride home. So we can't stay long."

"No problem. I've got some fresh coffee on, and I'll keep you just long enough to serve you a cup."

They walked inside and up a long corridor toward a series of offices. The shabbiness of the place was shocking even to Whittlesworth. The paint on the walls was smudged and the plaster cracked in places. Not a square yard of the fraying red carpet had all of its threads. Crisscrossing it like lines in a child's sidewalk game, duct tape ran across gaping tears.

"Whatever I've been sending, it obviously wasn't enough," Whittlesworth noted with a toothy smile.

"Oh, it was enough. We just didn't use it for maintenance. We thought the Diocese might do that. Of course, we were wrong. The Bishop's plan is to tear St. Andrew's down."

"Wait a minute." Whittlesworth stopped. "Are you part of this silent minority that Peter has going on the Plan?"

"I've always been a minority, Mr. Ash. Not so silent, but definitely a minority. Here, let's get your coffee, and let me give you a little refresher tour."

Whittlesworth gladly took the brew. He was far less thrilled with the prospect of a refresher tour. He stood for a second in Spencer's office, sipping at his mug. The office was even worse than the common spaces. Books and papers were stacked all around. An old leather couch had huge splits in all three of its green cushions. Two panes of glass had been replaced with plywood. The desk lamp was a wine jug with a cork fixture stuck in it. The office had the appearance of long-term deprivation. This wasn't the funkiness of an absentminded professor, but rather the dreary, almost desperate trappings of an individual or an organization whose belt had been tightened well beyond the promised moment of satiation. It was indeed a church under siege, and yet the back halls and the offices and every fixture they contained bore the appearance of survival. Given half a chance, Jim Spencer would win this war of attrition that was being fought.

"So . . . " Whittlesworth broke his silent reflections on St. Andrew's and the plight of its rector, "you were going to give me a tour."

"Yes. Of course. Well, come on down this hall." Spencer led them down a poorly lit back hall. Closed doors lined it on the right and the left.

"What's behind these doors? Offices?" Whittlesworth was curious about all the space and so little sign of its use.

"They were offices. We had an assistant rector, a choir director, church secretary, and even a bookkeeper."

"And?"

"And we had to lay them off."

"Look." Whittlesworth stopped just as they were entering the sanctuary. "How can a church run without music and someone to

answer the phones? Don't tell me you're an organist and a reception-
ist, too?"

Spencer laughed a big, deep, honest laugh—one that seemed to
emit an enjoyment of the struggle in which its owner was engaged.
"The organ broke three years ago. We lost the staff last year. But we
have music!"

"You play the harmonica or something?" Whittlesworth thought
he'd test Spencer's humor a little further. His answer was another
round of laughter.

"Close. I play the guitar for services with music."

They walked into the sanctuary, and Whittlesworth saw immediately that the problems in the rectory were only compounded in
the church itself. Pews were missing in spots. The carpet was worn
down to the pad, and the area lacked any pretense of attraction, with
one exception—the windows. Whittlesworth's eyes fixed on them,
stained glass of intricate beauty, showering the spartan interior of the
church in rainbows of red, yellow, and blue.

"Admiring your family's gifts, I see."

"Hmmm. Oh, the windows? Yes. Yes, of course."

"Each one," Jim Spencer counted from one end of the church to the
other, "given in the name of a child. Do you remember yours?"
Luckily Spencer was pointing at the window. Whittlesworth stared
at it. It portrayed the parable of the lost lamb. He wondered if it had
been given before or after his predecessor had moved away.

"Yes. Yes, I do indeed." Again, Whittlesworth didn't need any re-
quests for details. Better to switch the subject. "Okay, so my gifts go
for something else. Like what?"

"Ministering to the poor. The homeless. People who wander in
here from all around the city."

Why had it not occurred to him before? Had he so thoroughly
adopted the persona of another man that within twenty-four hours he
could not recognize the type of shelters where he had sought and
obtained a meal and a place to sleep? Men like Spencer had made his
life more bearable. In some instances, they had given back life to the
weaker of his fellow travelers.

"Jim has been fighting a pretty tough war here at St. Andrew's, Mr.
Ash." It was Peter again. He probably senses me wavering, Whit-
tlesworth thought. A potent and potential ally. That would never do.
To buck authority was to invite disaster. To encourage Peter and Jim
Spencer was to create more trouble for himself and everyone in the
hours and days to come.

"You know, Reverend Spencer, I guess these homeless types smell
pretty bad."

"Christ didn't smell the beggars and the cripples before he healed them."

"But," Whittlesworth knew he would prickle a nerve, but it was necessary, "you aren't Christ . . . and neither were your old parishioners. You're all just folks who don't like the smell of cheap wine and urine any more than the next guy."

"Hey, that's enough." Peter's face turned crimson.

"No wait, Peter. You're right, Mr. Ash. Maybe my zeal did outdistance my need for compromise. But we asked the bishop for money to renovate some space in the back. For some day quarters and to spiff up the old kitchen and cafeteria. Some areas where we could serve the poor—and not unduly shock our last few regulars. But it's the Bishop's plan to have this place razed in another six months. So he hasn't given a penny to St. Andrew's in a year or more."

"Well, why don't you ask my brother," Whittlesworth fumbled for a second over his name, "Thaddeus? After all, it's our stained glass hanging around here. Surely he appreciates that."

"Your brother, Mr. Ash, moved his letter out to St. Francis—in the suburbs—twenty years ago."

"Man of great foresight, Thaddeus." Whittlesworth's observation was made with as little commitment as possible. He had been straying for a moment with the Thaddeus suggestion. He must not stray. He must not become their ally.

Whittlesworth was ready to leave—to close his eyes to St. Andrew's and consider its plight unfortunate but unalterable. He turned just as the front door of the sanctuary swung open. A bright shaft of sunlight shone where the dark walnut door had been closed. All three men blinked, temporarily blinded.

"I'm sorry. I heard a guy could stop in here for a loan." Whittlesworth shrunk back instinctively. The voice was unmistakably Buddy's. Buddy, arriving out of nowhere to panhandle from some minister who barely had enough money to buy coffee. Whittlesworth felt a sudden wave of guilt. He had left Buddy the night before—left him carrying hundreds of dollars in the old man's wallet. But he hadn't even offered Buddy one of them. Whittlesworth's eyes grew accustomed to the light. Jim Spencer was instinctively reaching for his billfold.

"No, no, I insist," said Whittlesworth, stepping forward. "This is one small area where a member of the family can help his fellow man." Whittlesworth practically leaped to Buddy's side before Buddy could let out the gasp of surprise that Whittlesworth could see forming on his lips.

"Here you are, my good man." While Whittlesworth ostentatiously fished in his vest wallet, he whispered to Buddy in a voice that neither Spencer nor O'Malley could possibly hear. "Sorry I left you dry last night. Here's a hundred bucks."

"A hundred bucks!" Buddy boomed.

"Shhh . . . for God's sake . . . look, they got me. Police picked me up this morning. You were right."

"You bet I was right. You shouldn't have done it," Buddy whispered back.

"Save the lecture. Just listen up. I'll call you tonight or early tomorrow morning. Soon. Hang around the Mission."

"Okay."

"Now, see if you can't use that to try to lead a somewhat better life." Whittlesworth's voice became louder, deeper, and more authoritative. Spencer looked suddenly uplifted, less bedraggled. He had witnessed one of life's small miracles. Buddy slipped back through the door as quickly as he had appeared. In an instant it was almost as if he had never been there.

"Well, Jim, if bringing Mr. Ash here didn't accomplish any long-term conversion, at least he brought a little light into that old man's life," Peter said.

"Thank you, Mr. Ash. You are very generous. Very generous. Your ancestors would be proud." Spencer's voice was low, almost husky.

"Forget it. Listen, I've got to get going. Home or whatever." Whittlesworth felt odd—not uncomfortable, but far different than he had felt before. In that one instant standing in the sunlight with Buddy—even while he was planning his escape—he had experienced the most delicious feeling imaginable. He had the power to do exactly what he wanted to do—to give Buddy the money he had forgotten to give him the night before. The feeling was at once wonderful and eerie, fulfilling and disturbing.

"I'll see you soon, Mr. Ash."

"Yes. I'll look forward to it," Whittlesworth noted casually, not realizing just how soon it would be.

CHAPTER 8

The King of the Clan

"CAN WE GO now?" Whittlesworth settled uneasily in the front seat of Peter's Volkswagen. In less than twenty-four hours his life had been transformed from one of basic tranquility to one of turbulence. He had retreated from the tensions of a so-called rooted life years before. He didn't want it. He didn't need it. Yet now he had unwittingly entrapped himself in roots sufficient to strangle him.

"Yes. I'll take you home. They probably have the police out looking for you again." Peter's almost manic enthusiasm had subsided. He didn't notice Whittlesworth jump at the word "police." He had played his trump card of sympathy and failed—except perhaps on Whittlesworth's most personal level. The extravagant gift to the bum was gratifying, if somewhat wasteful. Peter had long ago subscribed to the philosophy that he would rather take one of those fellows to McDonald's for breakfast than listen to their line about bus fare to see their sick mother in Nashville. He was positive that Whittlesworth's generous gift would be wine by noon, although, at a buck a bottle, it ought to hold the guy for a while.

Whittlesworth sat equally subdued, resentment well-

ing up within him for the first time. For the past two hours he had known only the angst of uncertainty. Who would assault him with twenty questions next? Who would offer him bits and pieces of a past he knew only as a basically bare crazy quilt? With Peter's diversion to St. Andrew's the ante had been raised, the pace of the game quickened. Now he was supposed to be a savior of sorts, as well as a businessman and family member. It was too much to demand.

Hadn't he served his country like everybody else? Hadn't he fought in the war, been wounded, and picked up his medals? Hadn't he tried to go back home after the war, to undo all those years of riding the rails during the thirties? Hadn't he even finished up high school, an old man of thirty-two, and tried to start college on the G.I. Bill? Hadn't there been a girl? A girl with rich auburn hair and freckles that lasted all year round? A girl with sturdy shoulders and long legs who wanted to have children—lots of them. A girl that laughed so much she didn't have sense to get in out of a winter's rain. A girl who wouldn't stop chasing after life, even when she was so sick with pneumonia and the flu that anyone else would have been in the hospital. A girl who had died, for which he could never forgive her.

Whittlesworth shivered.

"Are you cold? Should I turn up the heat?"

"No," Whittlesworth snapped.

Where had the rest of life gone? One boxcar after another, making scratch from one town to the next. Picking oranges in Florida or Texas, apples in Maine or Michigan. Loading trucks, portering buses, lumbering, working with the circus. Years passing in clusters. Decades consumed one after another. Now here he was in a Volkswagen Bug with a fortune he couldn't spend.

They rode in silence—no chatty details about the park or the architecture or the wrought-iron lightposts or the bronze fountain. Just the steady but irregular rhythms of Peter's dying car. After all those years of freight cars and semis and even an occasional Greyhound, he was expending the luxury of auto travel in an antiquated Cadillac and a used-up Volkswagen. Whittlesworth shook his head. The Cadillac was better. He wished he were back in it.

"Well, I guess you're looking forward to seeing Helen again." The words came out of Peter's mouth in a completely innocent monotone. Images of the girl with auburn hair. No, her name was Ruth, not Helen.

"Who?"

"John's widow, Helen."

Whittlesworth readied himself for another terroristic jaunt down Peter's idea of memory lane. "Should I be?"

"Well," Peter hesitated, embarrassed, purposely avoiding Whittlesworth's intense stare, "you all were romantically involved, right?"

Whittlesworth reached for the door handle. Enough was enough. No, he couldn't do it. Peter was going almost thirty now.

"What makes you think Helen will remember that?"

"Oh, I've heard her mention you a time or two. Since John's death. She remembers." Whittlesworth was glad she did. Too bad he didn't. He spotted the mansion in the next block. He needed more information.

"What does she remember . . . that she's told you about?"

"Well, of course she was only fifteen or sixteen, and it was a long time ago."

"Right. But what? Indulge an old man's curiosity."

"Okay. She remembers summer dances in a gazebo over there on the edge of the park. She remembers Bing Crosby coming to town for a concert and the two of you walking home together. She remembers sitting on the porch swing and serving you lemonade."

"Well, I've tried to forget those times."

"She's said that you probably would."

Peter pulled the Volkswagen up in front of the house.

"Thaddeus is here."

"Hmmm?"

"The Mercedes." Peter pointed to the fire-engine-red sports car in front of his VW. Whittlesworth sunk down farther in the seat. Another harbinger of his doom. His purported brother would be part of the welcoming committee.

"Great."

Peter got out of the car and opened the passenger door for Whittlesworth. Whittlesworth swung first one leg, then the other onto the curb and stood upright. The end was at hand. The charade was nearly over. He had ceased thinking about the reasons and rationale behind his lemming-like drive for destruction. They no longer mattered. He was here. He felt almost detached. He would see it through. He would "be home." Just like the old man had said.

They moved up the walk together. Within moments he would be ushered back out the door under the able guidance of one of the city's finest. Now they would have their case. Officer Harter would have his reprise. Whittlesworth shuddered.

"This must be quite a moment for you."

"Right," was all that Whittlesworth could muster. He felt his knees weaken. Somehow he shuffled up the final set of steps. Peter was pulling the ancient doorbell. A distant bell was ringing. Figures were hurrying towards them, seen through the frosted, cut glass. The door was swinging open.

"Helen, I've brought Whittlesworth home." The king of the clan had arrived.

Silence. An attractive elderly woman stood before him in the doorway. She seemed to be looking right through him—an eerie, beguiling look. A look that denied any knowledge of his fraud. Her eyes were a beautiful blue-gray, but somehow empty, as if caught in a daydream.

"Whit?" The sudden appearance of a little girl, a pretty young woman in her mid- to late thirties, and an older, slightly overweight man hanging back from the others. "Whit?" the older woman repeated. Why the questioning tone? Why the odd expression? What was wrong?

"Whit?" she repeated. Then it flashed upon him. She couldn't see him. She was blind.

"Helen," he fumbled over her name. "Helen. It's been so long. It's . . . it's so good to see you."

Helen laughed. "I wish I could say the same."

"Oh, no, please, I'm sorry . . . "

"Whit, stop that. Oh, come on." She reached out her arms and he moved over slightly so that her embrace would not miss him. He felt the warm, soft touch of a woman for the first time in years. He shuddered. He could tell that she was crying. Over her shoulder he found himself staring into the eyes of the Ash family. He waited for someone to gasp and call for the police. But no one seemed surprised. What was wrong with them? Were they blind, too? "It's so good to have you home," she finally murmured.

"It's so good to . . . be home." What more could he say? What would he say next? They were all waiting. "And this is my," he paused to swallow, "family?"

Helen released her hold on him and turned around. "James Whittlesworth Ash, this is your brother, Thaddeus."

Thaddeus thrust forward from his position behind Jane and Katie. Whittlesworth looked him in the eye, ready to turn and run if he perceived even a hint of suspicion. Thaddeus showed only an undisguised awe. He held out his hand as he would have to greet a celebrity.

"Whittlesworth . . . I'm speechless. To meet you now . . . for the first time. . . ." In spite of himself Thaddeus was overwhelmed. More out of shock and a compelling need to do something than any other reason, Thaddeus hastily introduced Jane and Katie.

"You are a legend in your own time, Uncle Whittlesworth." Jane first held out her hand, then gave Whittlesworth a healthy squeeze. A different thrill than that felt from Helen's embrace. Jane was taut, electric, and carried an aroma of cigarette smoke and Chanel No. 5. "Welcome back," she said.

"And this is . . . " he strained for a second to remember the name neatly printed on the letter, ". . . Katie." Whittlesworth dropped to one knee and Katie instinctively jumped into his arms. A boy would have shied away, he thought. Little girls weren't so indecisive. Katie withdrew and looked wide-eyed and mystified into the face of her mythical great uncle.

"Yes, I know all about Katie," he said. He looked up and caught the look of puzzlement in Jane's eyes. She must not have known about Katie's letter. He leaned over and took Katie's hand, drawing her near to him. "You pen a fine letter," he said softly. Katie grinned, still muted by his presence.

Through all of this, Peter, feeling more out of place by the moment, had returned to the car to retrieve Whittlesworth's bags. He swung them through the front door and set them down in the front hall. Whittlesworth winced as the black bag fell over, but it had been securely clamped shut.

"Thank you, Peter." Jane was the first to stop staring, trance-like, at Whittlesworth. "If you would, maybe you could take those upstairs to the room next to Katie's . . . the guest room. Uncle Whittlesworth, we're sorry for the accommodations. The house has gotten a little run down."

"That's right, Whit. I told Helen and Jane that you'd probably want to stay out in Bellemonde with Sally and me."

"No. Not at all. This will be fine." He had to think fast. Stay close to downtown. Stay close to Buddy. Stay close to the Mission and the train yards less than two miles away. He had been temporarily lulled into a false sense of security. Anything could happen. Who knew how many old family friends were dressing up to come over at this very moment to spill the beans?

"But it's more comfortable, and a little newer, out at our house."

"No. I appreciate your offer, Thaddeus, but I'd kind of like to see the old place for awhile."

Thaddeus started twitching his nose and scratching at his right ear. Signs of high agitation. The last thing he wanted was for Whittlesworth to "see the old place for awhile."

"But Whit . . . you know the old place is falling apart, and pretty soon under the new Plan, I mean, you know," Thaddeus smacked his hands together, ". . . down she comes."

"No," Whittlesworth shook his head slowly, not wanting to let on

that Peter had told him anything, "I don't know anything about the
Plan, except for what your letter said."

"Well, it's a really excellent Plan . . . "

"That's your opinion, Thad," Jane interjected.

"Enough . . . enough . . . " Helen said gently. "No family politics
right now. Whit, you must be exhausted."

"I am. You can't imagine." Anything to extricate himself from the
front hallway and a sudden brouhaha in which he might be requested
to take sides.

"Katie, take Uncle Whit up to the guest room, will you,
sweetheart?"

"Sure, Grandma. Come on, Uncle Whittlesworth."

Peter passed them as he returned from the guest room, rejoining
the verbal battlefield. Halfway up the stairs, Whittlesworth could
hear Thaddeus and Jane exchanging short, staccato jabs while Peter
interposed grunts of encouragement. Whittlesworth quickened his
step. Escape. Escape out of their range of hearing. Out of the range
where they might ask some ridiculous and dangerous question. They
rounded the top of the stair and started down the long hallway which
ended in Katie's room. He examined the portraits on the wall closely.
So many of them looked like the old dead man left in the lot by the
Wayside Mission. None of them looked very much like him.

"In here, Uncle Whittlesworth. In here." Katie had come back and
taken him by the hand. He couldn't remember ever feeling a hand
that small within his own. He must have at some early stage in his
life. He had had a little sister once a long, long time before. But no
hand this small in the past sixty years at least.

"You'll sleep here. And you can put your clothes in those drawers,
and hang your coat in here . . . "

"Whoa, whoa, whoa, Katie." Whittlesworth held his palms in front
of him to slow her down. "I may be here a night or two . . . maybe.
Then I'm on my way. I've got to get along. Back, well, back to where I
came from."

Katie looked like she was going to cry. Whittlesworth didn't know
how to deal with this. It was a new development of another sort. He
had slid past Helen and Thaddeus with surprising ease. The last thing
he had expected was to be confronted with a tearful six-year-old. He
sat on the edge of the old, iron-frame bed and drew her to him. How
much could he promise to her without overstepping even his own
loose code of honor? Adults were one thing. If they wanted to fool
themselves into thinking he was their long-lost uncle, so be it. But
Katie was different. She was truly an innocent. Her education in

human frailty would begin soon enough. He had no desire to start the lessons.

"Katie . . . think of it this way. If you hadn't written to me, I wouldn't be here at all." It was a permissible lie. He had no idea what his predecessor had in mind when he started across the country. "I mean, Christmas morning comes for only a very short time." Whittlesworth tried to remember what Christmas morning was like. There were vague stirrings of excitement over gifts, fruits, and candies. "Then it's gone. My visit is like that. Let's try to make the time I've got here as good as we can. Then we'll have happy memories, and we won't waste all of our time wishing things were going to last longer."

Katie hesitated, but eventually acceded. "Okay."

"So, show me your room. In fact, show me all around the upstairs. It's . . . been a while." Whittlesworth knew that if he could cajole Katie into an activity of some sort, the newness of his being with her could be diffused.

So Katie took his hand and began the tour of the domain of the last child to play hide-and-seek in the Ash Mansion's long halls and interconnecting rooms. Katie's room was first, complete with a description of the wallpaper and her china dolls and her stuffed animals and even her books. Whittlesworth revelled in each moment. No quizzes about his past, no embarrassing probes into his life, no buttonholing over the issue of Thaddeus's Plan. Just an open adoration of an unknown but beloved great uncle. Katie provided the first and only real temptation of his new identity.

After Katie's room came her mother's, which Katie pointed out was Whittlesworth's old room, and which Whittlesworth pretended to recall. It was adorned even now with remnants of her own little girl and teenage years. Helen's room was next—neatly laid out and organized for Helen's sightless maneuvering. They left Helen's room, and he lingered again by the Ash family portraits.

"Katie?"

"Yes?"

"I don't see myself in this group of pictures and things." He hated to steal from her innocence, but he had to know everything he could about his past if he was going to ever be safely reunited with Buddy. Better that Katie show him than fail in front of Thaddeus or Jane or another adult. Katie looked long and hard with him. Like two sets of magnets their eyes were finally drawn to a photo of two boys and an older man. It was black and white and had as its background the front door of the Ash Mansion.

"That's my granddaddy." Katie's finger rested on the smaller, younger boy.

"The other boy's . . . uh, my . . . face has been scratched off or something." Whittlesworth knew it must be his predecessor. But he had no idea why the face had been obliterated. "Do you know why, Katie?"

Katie's lips pursed. She was trying to piece together her collective knowledge of family lore. Something she couldn't quite recall— something her six-year-old mind wasn't quite sure of yet. "No, I don't," she stated matter-of-factly. He would have to find out on his own. His attention turned from the little boy to the grown man.

"Why, Katie, that looks exactly like Thaddeus." The resemblance was almost exact—as if Thaddeus had gone to an amusement park and dressed in old clothes and pasted on a mustache for a joke portrait. It was a family resemblance if ever there was one, yet obviously this was Thaddeus's father or grandfather. Whittlesworth wondered what other secrets these fading black and white snapshots held.

"You're right, Uncle Whittlesworth." Katie's voice bore the awe of first-time comprehension. "It really does."

"Well, enough picture peering. If that's it for the tour, let's go on back downstairs to the adults."

"No, wait," she said, grabbing his arm. "Let's go and see the playroom."

"I thought we'd seen every room."

"It's upstairs—on the third floor. You remember. Come on." Her voice had an unmistakable yearning quality, much like Peter's had earlier. This was an invitation to a special place with special meanings.

"Okay." Whittlesworth smiled. "Why not?"

They started towards the rear of the house, past the top of the main stairway and back through the door into the back hallway. There, winding upwards, was another stairway, narrow and curved, less ornate than its counterpart leading to the front hallway, but more delicate and gracious—a fitting pathway to a magical place. Katie became very quiet, almost secretive in her mannerisms. They were entering mystical ground.

"Come on, let's go. We're going to be late." Thaddeus's voice boomed up the stairs. Whittlesworth turned to Katie and raised his eyebrows. Thaddeus was still very much in charge.

"Maybe another time, Katie?" He patted her on the shoulder.

"Okay," she said. Her disappointment was obvious. Her chin lowered and without protest she turned back around. Whittlesworth followed.

"We're going to be late. Come on!"

Whittlesworth and Katie stared down at Thaddeus from their post at the top of the main stairs. "What's the hurry?" Even as Whittlesworth questioned Thaddeus good-naturedly, he could feel his own mood turning colder, guarded, and more cautious.

"The meeting's at eleven. We'll be late as it is!"

"What meeting?" Whittlesworth asked suspiciously. Thaddeus continued to pace by the front door.

"The final board meeting for the Plan. We've got to get everything wrapped up today. Tomorrow's Christmas Eve, for God's sake!" Thaddeus's voice bore its usual edge, common to his family, but new and grating to Whittlesworth. It was the edge of impatience, of progress straining for release.

"But we were about to see the third floor," Whittlesworth chuckled.

"It's dirty up there. . . . " Something caught his eye as he looked back from his pacing to his older brother still standing on the first step. "My God, you didn't get ready. Do you have any idea who's going to be there?"

Whittlesworth's eyes narrowed. This stocky man who apparently held so much power was beginning to bother him. It was time to give him back a little of his own vitriol.

"Whoever it is, I suspect they'll accept me as I am!" It was a softly spoken growl. Whittlesworth prided himself on a toilet more closely kept than his other brethren of the road and the city streets. Besides, he had shaved and bathed just last night. The idea that one day's whiskery bristle and some straggling hair might offend Thaddeus or anyone else was new to him.

"Just remember, Uncle Whittlesworth—you're about to meet the elite," Jane quipped.

"I'll drive over in my car." Peter tucked his muffler inside of his tan corduroy jacket.

"How 'bout no car at all. You're not invited, Peter."

"It's a public meeting, Thaddeus. Peter can have his say." Helen pled Peter's cause while Thaddeus continued to shake his head and redden.

"It's only public because people like him," Thaddeus pointed an accusing finger at Peter, "insisted on slowing the process down by their participation."

"It's public because you need one-third of the project's cost to come from the taxpayers of this city!" Peter returned Thaddeus's bombast and now pointed his finger at Thaddeus.

"If you both don't watch it, your fingers are going to shake off your hands. If you want to come along, come with my blessings, Peter. I'd like to hear what you and your group have to say." Whittlesworth put forward his invitation more to gall Thaddeus than to join with Peter.

"You don't know what you're doing, encouraging him like this." Thaddeus's nose and cheeks were aflame.

"Maybe not . . . but I'd like to hear him." Whittlesworth's jaw set. He might have to go along with Thaddeus, but he didn't have to like it. He had known more than a few Thaddeuses in his life.

"Very well. We can't exclude you, O'Malley. But if you try any funny stuff, I'll call the police."

"At this point, I don't care what they do about the Plan." Jane stood on the living-room threshold smoking a cigarette. "But give 'em hell anyway, Peter. For old times' sake."

Peter turned abruptly. Was that a sign? A breakthrough? Maybe Jane was softening. He glanced back at Katie, yearning to make her his own again—to retrieve the rights that indecision and cowardice had robbed him of years before.

"For old times' sake." Peter winked, then turned and grabbed the handle of the front door. "Going with me, Mr. Ash?"

"He'll ride with me, Peter." Thaddeus's words were brittle, threatening to explode at any further provocation.

"I guess I'll try Thaddeus's car, Peter. Just for future reference in case I decide to trade in the old Caddy." Whittlesworth diffused their anger with his whimsy, biting his lip to stave off his own frustration, and biding his time to achieve an earlier break for freedom.

CHAPTER 9

Chairpersons of the Board

THE BOARD OF Ash Square Development clustered around Don Cartwright as drones would a queen bee. Cartwright was money, power, and the future. He was dynamic, young, and charismatic. Most importantly, Cartwright made them feel good. He made them feel that they were all part of something very important. He was a national celebrity in the circles they most valued. What he had brought to cities across the country he would now bring to them. He was part of things that counted. He epitomized the team of major players to which Thaddeus aspired membership.

Next to Cartwright sat Sally Ash, reveling in fame by association. And why not? It was her right. The Plan had been spawned by her more than five years before while seated beside Cartwright at dinner, much like today. Neither the dinner nor her positioning next to Cartwright had been happenstance. Sally had determined that her destiny was not to be ordinary. And life with Thaddeus in the backwater of their city had begun to be very ordinary. So she had approached her father—Thaddeus's senior by only ten years—about helping with a list of dinner guests for a very special affair she was planning. If her father weren't chairman of the First Citizen's Bank and Trust, she would never have garnered Don Cartwright's presence at her side. And absent that long-ago evening of tinkling glasses and laughter, there would have been no December 23 meeting of the board. Sally believed in fate, as long as it was carefully monitored and directed.

Thaddeus had played his part. He had been a yeoman. No hours too long, no work too demanding, no single task too unpleasant. The job of fighting his brother John and then unseating John's widow from the family estate was a prime example. He had done it without questions or complaint. When the final victory was won, and the intricate puzzle pieces in place, he would rightfully share in the spoils. Yet, after all, Thaddeus was still a yeoman, a lieutenant, and, when necessary, a messenger boy.

Sally eased back in the soft leather of one of the boardroom's chairs. Cartwright received the well wishes of the other board members, first to his right, then to his left. They came forward and genuflected to his seat of power. Sally smiled. Like all men, he was easily flattered. The more they smiled and bleated his praises, the more he preened and glowed.

Sally's mind wandered for a moment. Let him have his strokes. She knew that her constant and unwavering determination had many times been the salvation of the Plan, and the Plan, in turn, had been the salvation of her marriage. The children were getting older now, and so was Sally. She didn't dwell on it, but it was true. In another year or two—she was trying not to count—she would be forty. The men at the club would turn their heads less often, the tennis and golf pros would cease to flirt, becoming merely solicitous, the women in the Civic Association would start thinking of her as matronly. They were unwelcome changes, but unavoidable and even tolerable if she knew that she could make the opening of a new Broadway season, or go to Cannes, or Monte Carlo, or buy a new Jag or a designer gown or more fashionable jewelry.

She had thought all of these things were possible when she married Thaddeus. His family had by birth what she lacked. Yet she had also inherited her self-made father's appreciation for the main chance. This was her last opportunity to turn the Ash name into a strength rather than an albatross. If the Plan died, so did the marriage. The two were now symbiotic, their hearts and life blood inseparably intermingled.

While Sally sat amidst the buzz, ensconced in the glory of her schemes, dreams of future grandeur taking shape before her, Thaddeus watched from the other end of the table. He knew exactly what was happening. He knew exactly what Sally was thinking. The Plan needed to work. Its time had come. If that time passed, it would pass forever as far as he was concerned.

Sally was more winsome now than when they had married. Her features had transformed from the baby-fat beauty of the midwestern blonde to the more finely chiseled lines of a maturing cosmopolitan. From basic to classic, Sally had gotten better with age. But her appetite and tastes had refined as well. Her willingness to substitute or go without had all but vanished. Sally knew what she wanted, how to get it, and what to do if she didn't.

To his right sat the brother he had alternately idealized and excluded from his schemes for a newly defined family universe. Now this old man held the trump cards. Why had he invited him? What temporary insanity had prompted him to suggest his coming for Christmas rather than simply sending a proxy? Had this been his secret wish come true? The visit by a family member more wealthy and powerful than even Sally and her father could imagine? Was this his way of combating Sally's all-too-familiar implications that the Ash family genes were weak? If it was, Thaddeus had to laugh at his own folly. The man was practically enfeebled. Not physically, perhaps, as he had thought, but mentally. He was not a man capable of wielding the power of a multimillion-dollar empire.

"What are you thinking about, Whit?" Thaddeus had noticed the old man's almost hypnotic attentiveness to the western skyline. In a minute the meeting would begin. He had to get Whittlesworth's attention long enough to move the Plan to a final vote and execute the necessary papers.

"I'm thinking," Whittlesworth paused, "that there is snow in those clouds coming this way."

"So what? White Christmas, eh? Nice."

"I think it's going to be a pretty big snow. A killer."

"Well, don't you worry now, Whit. The mansion's withstood a lot of storms of all sorts since you left."

Whittlesworth turned to Thaddeus and smiled faintly. "I know that. I'm not thinking about myself. I'm thinking about all of the people on the road."

"There's traveler's rest stops. Their cars will get them there."

"What if they're not in a car?"

Thaddeus looked at him and sighed softly. Whatever was the old man talking about? Best humor him. "Yes. Yes, of course. I see. Well, after the board meeting, we can talk about that again."

Thaddeus looked around the table one last time. They were all there: Cartwright; Sally; the mayor; the mayor's head of development; Sally's father, Frank Grissle; Mrs. Jordan Albertson, inheritor of the news publishing empire; the bishop of the diocese; Ed Beech, legal counsel; and the president of the local carpenter's union. Money, labor, law, the electorate, and the free press. Thaddeus had chosen carefully. They had all stuck faithfully with the process. This was the payoff. Then he noted briefly the omissions: Peter O'Malley and his threatened demonstration of neighborhood opposition. Thaddeus couldn't help but take pleasure in their absence in this last moment before the Plan's final adoption.

"If we could all come to order in just a moment." A second passed while the assembled egos had their last words with Cartwright and settled back in their seats. "We have waited a long time for this wonderful moment. Here to share it with us, and home for the first time in over fifty years, is my brother, James Whittlesworth Ash."

There was immediate and apparently heartfelt applause. Thaddeus motioned for Whittlesworth to stand up. When he hesitated, Thaddeus started to help him up, but Whittlesworth twitched his fingers to wave him off and stood up to the applause. Just as he started to sit down, Thaddeus continued, motioning for him to remain standing. "I would like my brother—come back home from so far away and from so distant a time—to say a few words to us before this historic moment."

Speeches. The man was insufferable, Whittlesworth thought. It was bad enough that he remained constantly on the verge of discovery. Now he was supposed to gild the proverbial lily with witticisms or truisms or plagiarisms or something. Was anyone here supposed to know him? Apparently not.

"Well," Whittlesworth began, "I'm glad to be here with you. Sounds like my brother has everything well in hand. I'm all for it. Now, if I could just slip away . . . "

"No, no, no. You're a very necessary player today." Thaddeus was unceasing.

"You don't say?"

"I do say. But first, we thought you might like to see what the Plan entails. Ed, if you could draw the curtains over there. I'll flip on the switch here." The room immediately darkened as the overhead lights slowly dimmed and then shut off. "And we'll see what we've been all about."

Within seconds Whittlesworth found himself staring at a large white screen that had descended from the ceiling. A video projector flashed on and he was captive to a skillfully produced summary of the Plan and the glorious future for the city center which it ensured. Images shone, and the narrator's superlatives tripped from his tongue. There would be better housing for the displaced, new high-rise condos for the young, white-collar types, retail space for boutiques and amenities . . . an endless list.

The production ended, the lights flashed on, the curtains pulled. Thaddeus turned dramatically to Whittlesworth, still blinded by the sudden change in lighting.

"Whit, this is our case for a better future. We think it's the best possible case, and it's only going to come once. We take it now, or lose it forever." He paused, taking one last moment's satisfaction at the unexpected absence of Peter O'Malley. "Ed," he turned to the project's lawyer again, "if you will help my brother with the deeds and other closing documents, we can dispense with a formal motion for now and conclude the family's part of the closing. Don, do you have anything to add?"

Cartwright had been leaning on Sally's arm, sharing some particularly interesting tale, fully cognizant of Thaddeus's words but generally bored by the small-town exuberance. He turned towards Thaddeus and smiled.

"We're ready to start demolition right after Christmas."

Ed Beech was at his smoothest, helpful and solicitous to a fault. He reached inside of his coat pocket and withdrew his fountain pen for Whittlesworth's use.

"Mr. Ash, if I may. You need to sign here," he pointed to the first indicated *X* on the page, "and here," indicating again, "and finally initial right here."

Whittlesworth took the pen. It felt heavy and awkward in his hand. Everything was happening much too fast. Somehow he hadn't realized that he would be expected to sign something. Why had this moment not been foreseen? He had read all the words in Thaddeus's letter. He had known that Whittlesworth was in town to close a deal. But what was a closing? He had never been at a closing. He had never attended the shuffling of papers from one to another. He had never lived through the buzz and half-joking directions of a final conclusion to months and even years of preparation. The pen seemed to move of its own will towards the first indicated line. Then, as he actually placed the nib of the pen to paper, he froze. Something like an electric shock jolted through him. A simple but terrifying question was raised in his befuddled consciousness: Did anyone present know Whittlesworth's signature? Was this the one act that would betray him?

One of the two oversized oak doors of the conference room flew open. Peter O'Malley walked in with Jim Spencer at his side.

"Hold on there, Mr. Ash." Whittlesworth looked up and slowly eased the pen from the paper as he would his finger from a trigger.

"Nice trick, Thaddeus. Why didn't you just have your goons beat us up out on the street?"

"What are you talking about?" Thaddeus's voice was volcanic in its anger.

"The guards who've been holding us downstairs."

"What in the hell are you talking about? I don't know anything about any guards. I just know that you and Reverend Spencer are too late to ruin this Plan now. We're ready to act and we're going to act!"

"Somebody detained us downstairs . . . that's the only reason we weren't here thirty minutes ago." Peter's voice had lowered slightly as he determined, even through Thaddeus's anger, that Thaddeus was telling the truth.

Thaddeus sucked in a lungful of air. He turned slowly to Sally and caught her smile. "You and your father had the guards downstairs stop them?"

"You didn't want to be disturbed, did you, dear?" Sally's cheeks rose up in a perfectly drawn smile.

Thaddeus turned back to Peter and Jim Spencer.

"My apologies for the delay. That wasn't my idea." He shot a glance at Sally and then her father. "But the fact remains that it's too late to change things now."

"Three weeks ago you told us it was too early." Jim Spencer's baritone, honed on funerals and Sunday sermons, quieted the entire room.

"That was three weeks ago, Reverend Spencer, and now it's too late to change."

"Jim." It was the bishop's turn to assert his authority. "You'd best stick with things that are in your bailiwick."

"St. Andrew's is directly in my bailiwick, Bishop."

"If you aren't careful, it could quickly be placed outside your bailiwick."

"Now we're making threats in the name of the Lord?"

"This is business, Mr. Spencer," the bishop started to rise from his chair, "and in this case it happens to be the best business for the diocese as well as the center city!"

"If you worried as much about the people I serve in the name of God as you do your club memberships, Bishop, you might not find it so easy to sit at this table."

"Enough, Spencer."

"Gentlemen . . . gentlemen." Whittlesworth had been in too many barroom brawls to entertain another one at age seventy-five. "Things will wait a few minutes. Thaddeus, you yourself expected Peter to present his ideas—whether or not they were accepted—and I take it your father-in-law's bank security delayed Peter and Mr. Spencer's arrival . . . in an unforeseen fashion?"

"Well, yes. You've got a point there."

"Okay, then. Let's see what they've got in mind."

Thaddeus looked at his older brother in dismay, while with considerable relief Whittlesworth carefully laid the fountain pen down on the papers in front of him. Thaddeus rubbed his hand across his lips as if trying to erase a very bad taste from his mouth. He knew Whittlesworth was probably slipping, but he had at least expected the infamous old capitalist to know when to suppress the opposition.

"Go ahead, Peter. We're all ears."

Peter stepped to the display stand, where an artist's rendering of Ash Square Development hung in multicolored splendor. He unrolled a pen-and-ink sketch which he had prepared and clipped it to the board. With a pencil he started pointing to specific areas of the drawing while he spoke.

"You don't have to tear the entire neighborhood down to make it profitable. It will work if you save a lot, tear out a little here," Peter pointed at the worst of the commercial structures, "and here," another half dozen, low-slung buildings, "and let the people who are actually living there keep their homes." Peter turned around in time to catch Sally snickering and Don Cartwright suppressing a yawn. "You need retail space, but you need people living there, too. And you need a church to serve their needs, Bishop." The bishop looked down at his folded hands. "Right here you can create new playgrounds for the younger folks who will move in here with families, and these grand old houses over here can be renovated, not torn down." Once led by Cartwright's example, the remainder of the board started yawning and looking at their watches. "As for Mr. Cartwright's twin towers, if you must have them they can be built right here . . . and here . . . with parking beneath for every car within four blocks." Peter placed his pencil back into his vest pocket. "Well, that's my plan."

"And who is going to pay for *your* plan, Mr. O'Reilly?"

"O'Malley, Mr. Cartwheel."

"Cartwright."

"Oh, yeah. Well, *my* plan . . . and I get the threat . . . could be paid for with less of *somebody's* money, not the least of which is the taxpayer's, Mr. Mayor, because of tax benefits and some federal grants I know about."

"Mr. O'Malley, you are a little late with your "preserve the old buildings and claim tax credits" song. That stuff went out in the early eighties. I should know. I did my share of rehabs. They were

okay. But frankly, I'm just as glad they're kaput. I like new. Don't
you?"

"Not when it's second rate. And not when it's an excuse for rolling
over people."

Thaddeus immediately stood up and reclaimed the floor. The last
thing he needed was Peter O'Malley finally offending Don Cartwright enough to send him back on the early flight for Houston.

"If we are all ready, in spite of Peter's continued irrational opposition, I suggest that we formally move to adopt . . . "

"Excuse me, Thaddeus . . . " The almost meek voice at his side
startled him. It was Whittlesworth. "Some of Peter's suggestions
merit further consideration." He was thinking primarily of the haz-
ard presented by signing Thaddeus's documents. On the other hand,
not signing them might put him at crossed swords with Thaddeus.
That was a position to which Whittlesworth did not aspire. "I need to
wait. Let's get together again tomorrow. I don't think I can sign right
now."

"No," Thaddeus half demanded, half pleaded. "We can't wait."

"I'm waiting, Thaddeus. You can't just rush me into this thing."

"But Whit, Don Cartwright is leaving tonight. Tomorrow's
Christmas Eve. There's not time to wait."

"Let's meet again tomorrow morning. It won't be a long meeting. I
just want to sleep on it." Whittlesworth was firm, if imploring. He
needed time to get away and rejoin Buddy. One night would do it.
This was all more than he had bargained for. He'd done his part and
worlds more.

Thaddeus looked down, as ashamed of his mystery brother as he
had been of John. Both of them were cut from the same cloth. He
began to doubt his own resolve as he raised his eyes to an unhappy
array of faces.

"Don," Thaddeus begged him with his eyes and the pitch of his
voice, "could you stay overnight?"

Cartwright's jaw set and he stared at Whittlesworth. The old man
had something up his sleeve. He was known for tricks like this. He'd
heard about this man.

"I've got the option on this project, and I'm not going to let it slip
by. I'll meet you all tomorrow morning. Nine o'clock?"

"Fine . . . great . . . nine it is, Don. Everyone?" There was a less
than enthusiastic murmur of eventual assent.

Everyone but Sally immediately stood up and exited. She sat staring coldly at Thaddeus and Whittlesworth ineffectually sputtering at
each other at the other end of the conference table. Peter whispered
something to Jim Spencer and then approached Whittlesworth.

"Thanks for the breathing room, Mr. Ash. Want a ride home?"

Whittlesworth realized he was walking a very thin tightrope. In order to keep his balance, he needed to swing ever so lightly back towards Thaddeus.

"Thank you, Peter. But I came with Thaddeus. I'll leave with Thaddeus. If that's okay?"

Thaddeus watched Sally as she slowly stood up, smoothed her dress, raised her eyebrows as if to question what had gone wrong, and left the room without another word. He turned back to Whittlesworth.

"Of course . . . I'd be glad to, Whit . . . of course."

CHAPTER 10

Katie's Playroom

WITH THE AFTERNOON came the temporary peace of a new-fallen snow. It started just as Thaddeus was driving with Whittlesworth from the parking garage. It was careening around them in thick clumps by the time they reached home, and by two o'clock the city had declared Operation Snowfall in full swing. All employees were sent home; all businesses closed. It was the perfect send-off for the last workday before the holiday.

The silence of snow brought the silencing of tongues. During their short drive, Thaddeus sat hunched over the creme-colored steering wheel of his 450 SL, while Whittlesworth kept his nose within an inch of the passenger's window. Over fifty years of separation and they had nothing to say. Or perhaps they had too much to say, thus choosing silence. Thaddeus wanted nothing more than to be done with the entire Christmas season. Whittlesworth wanted nothing more than to be free again.

In his pitiful Volkswagen, Peter drove Jim Spencer back to St. Andrew's in the silence of despair. They had been effectively shut out, their hopes for a breakthrough snuffed. Whittlesworth's intercession was far too little, far too late. The neighborhood support they had garnered weeks and even months before had dwindled to their own two voices. Not enough to get the newspaper's attention. Certainly not enough to get the attention of Thaddeus or Sally or Don Cartwright. They were just sufficiently impotent to be unlawfully detained by Sally's father's security police without any particular hue or outcry as to their civil rights. At least Thaddeus had apologized.

Peter drove to the front of the church, and Spencer jumped out.

"Thanks, Peter. I think you gave it your best shot."

"Which wasn't enough. And hasn't been enough for more than a few years."

"Ah, don't let it get you down." Spencer started to close the door, then stopped. "By the way, you don't have to come tomorrow night. It was just a crazy idea I had about a midnight service for the neighborhood."

Peter smiled, his zeal, but not his sincerity, depleted. "I'll be here, Jim. 'Lasts' are almost as important as 'firsts.'"

"Maybe so, Peter. God bless." Spencer slammed the door shut, and Peter departed.

Jane and Helen worked together around the long, three-pedestal dining room table, unloading linens, china, and silverware like thieves in the night, speaking in short, choppy sentences, their voices hushed. No one had reported to them from the front lines of the boardroom, but they somehow sensed that peace on earth and goodwill between the men of the Ash family had been upset. It was just a feeling, their intuition that things had not been ironed out.

Katie appeared in the door to the dining room, the only member of the family with anything approaching spirit. Her voice sparkled, too filled with expectation to be suppressed by her mother and grandmother's graveyard demeanor.

"It sure is quiet around here!"

Jane and Helen turned in unison with a simultaneous "Shhh!", then almost as quickly broke into laughter.

"You're right, Katie." Jane stroked Katie's hair. "It's too quiet in here."

"So let's make some noise! Put on some records, play the piano!"

The front door opened with a boom and slammed a second later with a pronounced bang.

"I think, honey, we had better chill out on the music and stuff for a while."

Thaddeus appeared at the dining room door. Behind him Whittlesworth sulked off to the parlor. Thaddeus's usual frown had deepened into a scowl.

"Well, we wasted *this* morning!"

"Meaning your board didn't approve the Plan?" Helen asked.

"Meaning Whittlesworth," Thaddeus's voice became hushed as he jerked his head towards the parlor, "turned out to be as spineless and indecisive as . . . " Thaddeus contained his anger.

". . . as my father?" Jane completed his sentence.

"No . . . " Thaddeus lied, "No. I was going to say . . . well . . . what does it matter what I was going to say?"

"You're right, Thad," Helen interjected, "it doesn't matter what you were going to say. What happened?"

"Peter and the padre showed up at the last minute. They confused the old man and he asked for another day to think it over."

"A reprieve from the governor!" Jane mocked.

"You'll have your reprieve in limbo if Cartwright gets on that jet tomorrow without signing off on the plan."

"Well, worse things could happen," Jane noted with practiced nonchalance.

"I give up!"

"When are Sally and the children coming over?" Helen had gone back to the business of setting the table.

"Sally will have to disengage herself from Don Cartwright first. Mr. Charm! Then Thad Jr. will have to force himself away from the Eastern Mall and his cadre of juvenile delinquents long enough to pick up Sadie at her girlfriend's house. If all goes well, they should pour in here about five. Whenever it is, it will be too soon."

"Ah, fatherhood! Love in its purest form."

"One could say that." Thaddeus shook his head. "I wouldn't. But one could say that. I'm joining Whittlesworth."

Thaddeus followed his own resolve, taking the opposite wing chair from his brother by the fireplace. For a second they acted as if the other were not present. Whittlesworth looked down at his hands. Thaddeus looked upwards as if fascinating hieroglyphics were dancing across the ceiling. They both cleared their throats. Neither spoke.

"Can I get either of you a drink? Bourbon? Scotch?" Jane stood at the door, bemused by their mutual discomfort.

"Well," Whittlesworth licked his lips. One good, stiff drink might settle his head a little. "Maybe I might have a . . . "

"It's too early in the day for liquor." Thaddeus's pronouncement was made without regard for anything Whittlesworth was about to say. "I'll have some coffee."

"Yes, coffee would be fine." Whittlesworth's senses rebelled at the idea of hot coffee when quality bourbon was being offered, but he needed to go along, in this case to get along and out the door.

Jane leaned over and picked up a cigarette from the case on the side table. Her will to curb the habit had faded over the past weeks.

Whittlesworth's eyes tracked to the humidor that had belonged to John.

"I'm sorry, Uncle Whittlesworth." Jane had followed his glance. "Would you like a cigar? I think they're probably still fresh . . . "

"Nasty, filthy habit," Thaddeus interjected. "We banned smoking from our offices last September."

Whittlesworth clenched and unclenched his fists once before declining. He hadn't had a decent cigar in over twenty years.

"Thanks anyway."

"Suit yourself."

"Easier said than done, my dear," Whittlesworth murmured to himself.

"What?" Thaddeus asked.

"Er . . . easier fought than won . . . breaking the smoking habit, I mean."

"Yes. I see. Yes." Thaddeus's mumbling ended the exchange. Jane left the room and the somber, gray quality of the afternoon reasserted itself. A minute passed, then five, and the mantel clock sounded the half hour with a loud gong. Whittlesworth started.

"Hah!" Finally Thaddeus was paying attention. "You, too! When I was a little boy I used to jump every time that clock sounded."

"You were a little boy?" Whittlesworth's question hadn't come out as he intended, but it certainly indicated what he was thinking. "I mean, I just can't picture you as a little boy. Here in the same house where I . . . was a little boy."

"Yes." Thaddeus stared about him as if it were suddenly a different house than it had been just moments before. "I grew up here alone, really. You had John. It must have been nice having a kid brother to bum around with. With me, well, John was so much older. And you . . . I mean, you were already a legend by the time I was ten! Of course, by that time Dad was dead."

"Legends are hard models to live up to, Thaddeus. Especially when they're still alive."

"Yes. Well, sometimes they're all we have." Thaddeus eyed his older brother, surprised. His humility was unexpected.

"All right, here's your coffee. Next round you're on your own." Jane set the silver tray on the long walnut library table behind the sofa. She began to pour from the tarnished pot. "Cream, Uncle Whit?"

"Cream?" How long had it been since someone offered him cream? "Oh, yes. Yes, please."

Jane accidentally overfilled the cup. Whittlesworth reached for it carefully, placing one hand on either side of the saucer. A sudden slam of the door shook the walls. The chandelier overhead started swinging gently. Whittlesworth's hold shifted and coffee sloshed on the chintz upholstery. Whittlesworth murmured, "I'm sorry" just as Thaddeus leapt up and Peter entered the parlor. He had a wild look in his eyes, and the rapidity of his words reminded Thaddeus of Peter's drinking days.

"Well, you didn't give us a chance, Thaddeus!"

"There wasn't a chance to give you, Peter. Why should I waste my time? The board's mind is made up." The two were immediately eye to eye.

"Made up by what you spoon feed them. We deserve more of a hearing. You owe it to Helen and Jane and Katie if nobody else!"

"Please, no special pleas for the ladies of the house!" Jane's sarcasm had not softened. Whittlesworth stared at her. Wasn't this her home as well? Hadn't she grown up here, too? Why did it mean so little to her? In a way her response made him feel better. If forced to a position before the evening, he would find it easier to side with Thaddeus.

"I think you've been drinking!" Thaddeus's voice reverberated with accusation. Jane's glare was delivered with even greater effect. Peter started to present his defense to her, then gritted his teeth and snapped at Thaddeus instead.

"I stopped down at the Wooden Nickel. So what!"

"And you want the board to trust *you*? Old habits die hard, Peter."

"You should know," Peter countercharged. "Maybe a little booze would loosen us all up enough to be more honest with each other!"

"Well, it's a cinch we couldn't talk any louder!" Helen had heard the commotion, left the kitchen, and, grabbing Katie's hand, had come to the parlor. Her left hand, possessing the sensitivity of eyes, felt along the familiar surfaces of tables and chairs.

"Can we go to the playroom now, Uncle Whittlesworth?" Katie had her own agenda for the afternoon, but she also felt the older man's need for succor.

"I'll say!" Whittlesworth took a quick gulp of his coffee and abruptly set the cup down.

"Grandma?" Katie's age did not prevent her from being sensitive to Helen's needs. "Is it okay?"

"By all means, Katie. I'd think Whit could use a little relief from the adults in our family." Katie's hand slipped from Helen's. Thaddeus and Peter resumed their heated review of the morning's meeting, sharply disagreeing on the wisdom or futility of Peter's attending the final meeting to come. Jane watched them in frustration, wondering why she had ever returned from Boston, why she had ever let

Peter inch back into her life. Whittlesworth quietly exited their company.

Katie took Whittlesworth's hand and started up the stairs. For an instant he withdrew from Katie's touch. Her constant hunger for affection made him uncomfortable. Years on the road with little contact with children had made them objects of curiosity, but never the subject of emotion. They were simply observed from a distance, idly, as one might look at scenery from a passing train.

"Just a second, Katie." Whittlesworth detained his eager hostess long enough to approach Helen. He took her hand in his.

"Thanks for the breather, Helen."

A question mark of a smile trailed across her lips. "You know, Whit, it's been so long—but you just don't sound the same as you did."

Whittlesworth's palms turned icy. He could remember distinctly the voice of the old man less than twenty-four hours before: "Go . . . home." A higher-pitched voice than his own, a slight Southern accent still apparent.

"Voices change, Helen. It's been a long time. The West pounded out my accent."

"Yes. Of course. You're right." But Helen's expression belied her compliance—the boldly honest questioning of the blind. Her uncertainty remained. Whittlesworth's hand grew clammier and she noticed this as well. "Is something wrong, Whit?"

"No. No, not at all. I need to get going, though . . . eh . . . with Katie. Let's catch up later tonight, Helen. What do you say?"

Whittlesworth's legs wobbled as he and Katie climbed the two sets of stairs to the third-floor playroom. Not fatigue, but fear made them feel like rags. He took a breath as they mounted the last few steps. New resolve. New determination. Helen's simple query had set off another wave of paranoia. More than ever before he knew it was time to cut short his little charade. He had gone home for the old man and he didn't like it. Now it was time for *him* to go home—even home to the comforting nirvana of soup kitchens and open fires, innocent panhandling, and hard labor.

"We're here." Katie reached the top of the stairs, then turned to Whittlesworth with an impish smile. Finally it was her time and place. Three doors led from the third-floor landing, and with a dramatic flourish Katie swung open the one situated in the back of the house. She motioned for him to go first and he complied.

Walking into the long, narrow room was like stepping into another house—another world. Situated between two gables, the roof slanted and took odd angles, not anything like the spacious squared-off rooms on the first and second floors. Whittlesworth realized immediately that this was a room almost exclusively for children, cosy and closed. The ceiling formed a triangle with the floor and wall. Shafts of light flooded through the long, narrow windows, dissecting the room into three sections. The wallpaper was old and peeling in spots, patterned more for little boys than little girls, but meant for children in any event. There was only one other door than the one through which they entered. It was a four-foot miniature of the doors throughout the house, but more to a child's scale, probably leading to a closet.

In one corner was a dollhouse and a doll bed, and in the corner next to them was a collection of the dolls who resided within the room. At the opposite end of the room there was an ancient wooden rocking horse, its white, red, and yellow paint faded, but enduring. Next to the rocking horse there were dozens of toy soldiers and the remnants of an electric train. A bookshelf burst with old, slim volumes that spanned fifty years or more of children's tales. Throughout the room there was a clutter that beckoned to the childlike spirit in Katie and Whittlesworth and anyone who willingly stepped across its threshold. For a moment Whittlesworth simply stood there, hunched over, his hands on his thighs, taking in yet another facet of this new-found family of his.

"Do you remember?" Katie asked. It was a simple question. Whittlesworth's response was equally simple.

"Yes." And he did remember. Not this room, but another one, in another house, enjoyed and beloved by other children. There were universal truths contained within this room's multitude of walls. Its nooks and crannies called out across the limits of time and geography and clan. It was every child's hideaway.

"Will you play with me?" Katie asked. Without waiting for an answer she went directly to her dolls, taking one up and handing it to Whittlesworth. Whittlesworth wondered for a moment who in this family did play with Katie. Not Thaddeus for sure, nor her grandmother, limited by age and blindness. Not Jane, who was lost in her own personal crises, nor Peter, lost with Jane in the crises over the role he no longer played in her life or Katie's. No one.

"I'll bet John played with you up here." Whittlesworth's words merely searched for affirmation of what he sensed to be true. He answered Katie's question more simply by accepting the doll and sitting down.

"It was my granddaddy's playroom—and yours. Right?" Whittlesworth had followed Katie's lead and begun to dress the underclad baby doll.

"Yes. Yes, it was all of ours," Whittlesworth noted. Katie's eyes revealed her puzzlement. She was thinking.

"Do you mean Great Uncle Thaddeus, too?"

"Well," Whittlesworth pondered her question as he slipped the doll's tiny shoes over its feet, "I don't know. I wasn't here then."

"I was." The voice came from the third-floor landing. It belonged to Thaddeus and it startled them. "That's right, Katie. I'm sure no one has told you. I know I haven't. But I was the last to really use this room. Well, before your mother came along, anyway."

Whittlesworth noticed that for the first time Thaddeus was not scowling. It wasn't permanent after all. Instead, it had dissolved into a small smile that didn't fade after Thaddeus's comment.

"Well, have a seat, brother. There's dolls enough to go around for everyone!"

"I can't."

"You can't? You're younger than me. Your back and legs should hold up better than mine. Have a seat!"

"Well, I don't know."

"Oh, sit down." Whittlesworth's soft command seemed a faint and slightly mocking imitation of Thaddeus himself.

"Well, okay. But only for a minute." Thaddeus came to Katie's end of the room and squeezed his stubby frame under the dormer roof. He sighed and seemed contented to watch for awhile.

"Here," Whittlesworth said, handing him a baby doll, "make yourself useful. These babies need some love and care."

"I don't know. I mean, I just came up to check on you . . . "

"Okay. So you've checked on me. I'm just as loony as you thought. Now get to work."

Thaddeus shrugged and followed his older brother's lead. There was no one present to report on his actions or to record his play. He felt silly at first—very silly. But after awhile, it no longer mattered.

The light outside began to dim as the day wore on and the snowfall increased, brushing across the windows and then settling in concave mounds on the windowsills outside. Katie talked to the dolls or to her great uncles. The distinctions between the animate and inanimate blurred. The minds of the two older men drifted off in variant directions.

Whittlesworth's thoughts turned to a white, three-story frame house in the flat Ohio farmlands. There was snow there, too. Deep, midwestern snow. The glory of sledding on the county's one decent hill. Cold, oppressive snow, and the crush of the Depression, and the seductive, lonely wail of the midnight freight clattering south.

Thaddeus's wanderings ranged only across the narrow room. Allied toy soldiers arrayed against the evil forces of the Nazis. Cannon and battlement standing bravely. The chug of his Lionel winding its way in and about paper-mache mountains. The long winter afternoons spent alone, lost in a boy's delusions of grandeur.

"Thad! Are you up there, Thad? Answer me!" His mother? Thaddeus crossed back over barriers of time and space. No, his mother was long dead. The voice repeated. It was Sally announcing her hegemony over the house.

Thaddeus jumped up too quickly. His head thudded against the soft plaster of the slanted ceiling.

"Ouch!" Thaddeus winced. "Yes. I'm here. Coming!"

"Why didn't you answer me when I called?" Sally was standing in the doorway, her eyebrows arched at the unlikely and unorthodox sight of two older men apparently engrossed in dressing baby dolls. Thaddeus delicately lowered the doll in his hands, then tried to slip it behind his back.

"What are you doing?" Sally's question was as much an accusation. She was convinced that they were both batty. Thaddeus looked immediately to Whittlesworth and Katie for help.

"I was . . . rather . . . we were . . . well, you see . . . "

"I asked Uncle Thaddeus to play and he was playing." Katie looked serenely but with supreme resolve at her "Great Aunt" Sally. Sally stared back. This little girl would be formidable one day, she thought.

"If you must know, uh . . . " Whittlesworth fumbled over her name.

"Sally. We met briefly at the board meeting."

"Yes. Sally. I certainly remember the face, but not the name." Whittlesworth winked at her. "Thaddeus and I were just discussing the future of the Plan, and whether to start with the house, or the park across the street."

Thaddeus sighed with relief. Any irony or intended humor in Whittlesworth's remark was lost. It saved face, and for that Thaddeus was thankful. Sally had never played dolls in Katie's special room, nor seen the little light on the train locomotive piercing the darkness decades before. She didn't care. Thaddeus cared, but his caring had long since yielded to reality.

CHAPTER 11

The Guests Arrive

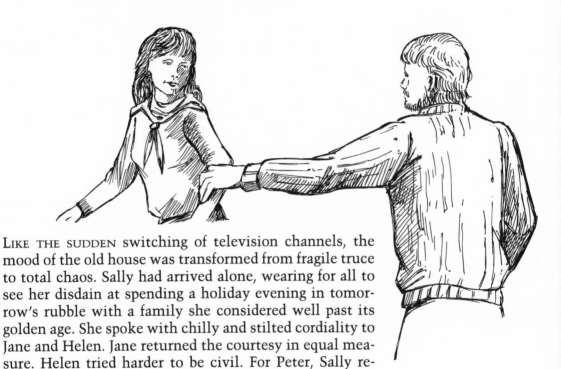

LIKE THE SUDDEN switching of television channels, the mood of the old house was transformed from fragile truce to total chaos. Sally had arrived alone, wearing for all to see her disdain at spending a holiday evening in tomorrow's rubble with a family she considered well past its golden age. She spoke with chilly and stilted cordiality to Jane and Helen. Jane returned the courtesy in equal measure. Helen tried harder to be civil. For Peter, Sally reserved her most direct venom.

"Do you realize you may have jeopardized the future of the city *and* the people you claim to represent?"

"Hello, Sally. It's good to see you again, too." Peter smiled.

"Don't waste your sarcasm."

"Okay. As a matter of fact I haven't jeopardized anything." Peter's tone was subdued and sober, the heat of his exchange with Thaddeus spent.

"Don Cartwright is ready to scrap the whole thing, and you haven't jeopardized anything?"

"If the Plan can't withstand a few concerned voices, then it's not very sound."

"You simply don't have any idea of the sensitivity of these negotiations, do you?" It was a rhetorical question and she neither required nor allowed response. "Where's Thaddeus?"

Jane referred her to the upstairs and Sally exited to retrieve her wayward spouse. The minute Thaddeus, Katie, and Whittlesworth returned, the doorbell rang again.

"I'll get it," Katie cried out.

She swung the massive door inward and found herself face to face with the two teenagers Katie knew only passingly as her second cousins. Thad Jr. walked directly past her without a word. Sadie gave what looked and sounded like a loud sniffle, followed by a bored look. Urchin of the poor side of the Ash family and waif of the inner city— these were Sadie's assessments of Katie.

"Thad! Sadie! I thought you weren't going to make it!" Thaddeus rushed to his children as if they were prodigals. They ducked his outstretched arms and started for the television in the den. Thaddeus grabbed Thad Jr. in his right hand and Sadie in his left. "Now, hold on a minute. There's someone I want you to meet. A very special person who . . . "

"Your rich brother, right?" Thad Jr. interrupted.

"Your uncle." Thaddeus's voice promptly regained the combative edge for which he was best known.

"He looks old enough to be my grandfather," Sadie added.

Whittlesworth eyed them with the enthusiasm of a mailman confronting the Doberman on a new delivery route. Thad Jr. didn't offer even the thinnest veneer of pleasantry. The earphones of his Walkman were resting on the back of his neck, and immediately after he limply accepted Whittlesworth's hand, they were brought into place and the Walkman turned on. Sadie emitted an air of unbearable boredom.

"Nice earrings," Whittlesworth commented dryly on the set of three gold hoops which pierced each of her ears.

"Yeah."

"Should've gotten one in your nose to match."

Sadie cocked her head, wondering at his prescience. "I tried. Sally cut off my allowance."

Sally cut off my allowance? Whittlesworth wondered. Whatever happened to "mom?" Who or what were these creatures that had suddenly been consigned to him?

"I suppose you call . . . uh . . . my brother Thaddeus?"

"No, I call him the 'old man.' 'Cause he is . . . old."

"How charming." Whittlesworth didn't like her. He not only didn't like her, he wanted to spank her and hang her by her earrings from the upstairs shower rod. But he checked his irritation and ill feelings and tried to imagine leaving town soon.

"Well, Whit, I know we all want to get to know each other better. Kids, I want you to get to know your uncle." Thaddeus stopped. His son had done an about-face and headed for the den. "Thad, come back here." The boy was a temporary deaf mute, gladly oblivious to his father's solicitations. Thaddeus stormed after him.

"You really live by yourself . . . all holed up in some penthouse?" Sadie's curiosity was finally aroused.

"When I'm not surrounded by a harem of young women." Whittlesworth's statement was made with poker-faced control.

"Really?" Sadie's eyes lost their sleepy, half-lidded appearance.

"It's just one constant party," Whittlesworth paused, "if you know what I mean." He didn't know what he meant, so he had no idea how she could. But she seemed to anyway.

"Unbelievable . . . " she muttered.

"Yes, I would say so." Whittlesworth smiled, now convinced that the extra puncture wounds in her ears had somehow permitted her brains to seep out. Without another word he wheeled around and returned to the parlor.

"Okay now," Thaddeus was saying between gritted teeth, "we're going to make this a nice visit in the parlor together." He looked intensely at Thad Jr., who was still wincing from the grip of Thaddeus's clenched fingers on his forearm. "Aren't we?"

"Yeah, yeah, get off me. Come on." Thaddeus plopped his son into the wing chair opposite Whittlesworth. Whittlesworth faced the boy as he had faced his father more than an hour before.

"So." Thad Jr. looked to see if he was still being monitored. He was. "You live in Colorado, eh?"

"Yep." Whittlesworth liked this kid even less than his sister. From his army fatigues to his shaven head, the juvenile had no apparent respect for anything or anyone.

"It must snow a lot in Colorado."

"Yep." Whittlesworth thought he might give him a second chance. "One winter I spent in the Rockies . . . "

"Do you, uh, ski?" Thaddeus's progeny had all of his father's bad traits.

Whittlesworth stared at the boy for a minute to determine if he was serious. Maybe he should be flattered if Thad Jr. thought he could ski at his age.

"Only the steep slopes. At my age you don't waste time on the middling mountains. One fall, steep or not . . . " Whittlesworth brought his hands together with a clap. Thad Jr. and Sadie both jumped. "And you're dead. At my advanced age, that is."

A minute passed. Two. Then five. Thad Jr. looked around and

confirmed that his father was off somewhere, probably arguing with his mother. Without another word he stood up, made a guttural noise that sounded like "goose creek" but which Whittlesworth finally interpreted as a garbled and primitive version of "excuse me," and left the room. Sadie, who had been staring vacantly at a blank wall, followed him.

Thaddeus's offspring had no sooner departed than Katie dared to reappear. She had been watching from one of her stairway vantage points, peering through the spindles and the open parlor door. Without a word she came up to Whittlesworth and waited. He had really never been around little girls—except his aunt's daughters years and years before—yet he instinctively knew what was expected of him. He reached down and nestled her on his lap.

"They aren't very nice, are they?" Katie was direct.

"No, they're not." Whittlesworth was equally direct. "But they might come out of it. Sort of like a coma, or a bad case of the flu."

Katie could no longer contain herself. Since Uncle Whittlesworth had walked into the house she had been desperate to know what effect her letter had had on him.

"Have you read my letter to you?" She knew by his first words to her that morning that he had, but she wanted to hear it again.

He paused, wondering to what extent he was willing to prevaricate with this little girl. "Many times, Katie. Many times." Katie smiled. "It was a secret letter, wasn't it?"

"Oh, yes!" Katie responded. "Don't tell anyone. Just you and me."

"That's a deal."

Katie grew bold, knowing that she was about to venture into an area that made Thaddeus livid and upset her grandmother, but forged ahead anyway.

"Have you made up your mind about our house?"

Whittlesworth said nothing for a moment. "No, I haven't. But I understand that your grandma, your mom, and you will all make a bundle of money if the Plan goes through. Is Helen against it?" Whittlesworth still wasn't sure of the family alignments on the whole affair.

"Yes. For sure. Grandma doesn't want to move from her home."

"And your mom?"

Katie had to think. "I don't think she knows. She says she doesn't care what they do, but I don't think she means it."

"I don't mean to pry, but I might as well. Are your mother and Peter engaged now?"

"Oh, no! They used to be or something. I'm not supposed to know anything about it."

Whittlesworth's lips rose in a smile of deep admiration. This kid had grit.

They were silent for a few minutes. Whittlesworth finally asked, "Why aren't your mother and grandmother at these Plan meetings?"

"Thaddeus doesn't want them there. Does he want you there?"

"Yes."

"Why?"

Whittlesworth thought. "I don't know for sure. I suppose to sign the deal and make it happen."

"Will you?"

Whittlesworth opened his mouth to speak, but was silent. Katie had truly caught him off guard for the first time during his brief visit. "I don't know. I really don't. Your Uncle Thaddeus seems to have things pretty well set and ready to go. A lot of good things could happen."

Katie stared at her great uncle and doubted for the first time whether her own dreams were going to come true. Right now he didn't seem at all like her Grandpa John. She sighed, then rested her head on his chest as they both watched the snow mounting outside.

Peter caught Jane as she was darting into the upstairs bathroom.

"Where are you going?" He knew it was a stupid question the minute it was asked.

"I thought I might take a little nap in the bath tub."

"I'm sorry. Dumb question. I just wanted to ask you something. And this is the first time I've caught you alone."

Jane reversed course and met Peter beneath a portrait of her father.

"Jane, I want to be a part of you and Katie's lives again."

"Peter, we settled all of that at the time of the divorce."

"But you wanted it that way. You weren't ever coming back."

"Things change."

"Exactly. Things change. People change. Circumstances change."

"Look, I never said things were *all* your fault. I just said that given what was going on in our lives, and in your life in particular, Katie would be better off growing up with no father than with you."

"Don't sugarcoat things now, Jane." Peter pursed his lips and held fast to his humor. Jane laughed, a breakthrough of immense proportions.

Peter started again, encouraged. "Maybe you were right. Then. Things were going very badly. We both know now that I had problems. At the time I didn't know it. After you and Katie left I got help."

"And when things went badly this morning, what did you do?" Jane's brooding anger finally bubbled forth. "I'll tell you what you did. You went down to the Wooden Nickel and you did what you always did . . . "

"No, I didn't."

"You did, Peter."

"No!" Peter's intonation grew stronger, and he started to grasp her shoulders. Then he stopped. Things could change. People could change. He had to believe that. He had to make Jane believe that. "I didn't do what I always did. Thaddeus may have thought it. I may have let him. But I didn't even have a beer. Not one. Seven years ago I would have still been there, falling off my bar stool and telling the barkeep how great I was and how awful the world was. But I didn't do that."

"I'll bet you started to."

"But I didn't. You can't take that from me. I'm here and I've been here. That makes it different from the old days."

Jane looked into his eyes in search of his soul. Peter would never truly grow up. But maybe he shouldn't. Maybe that was what endeared him to her and to everyone else who had given him a second chance. His spiritual essence was hope, blind faith, and dogged determination. Irish to the core. Strip him of that and one stripped his soul of personality, his heart of passion. He would always be what he was, and that included the lost cause, the flicker of chance, the long shot, and the tough odds. He might lose, but he would try again. And he would succeed often enough to demonstrate his worth.

Jane took his bearded cheeks in her palms and drew him to her. Their lips met for a second, then several. They parted, eyes closed.

"I love you, Peter," she said. He started to say something but she stopped him with a finger to his lips. "And I'll give it a chance. But that's all. No promises. No major changes. Take it slow. Wait and see."

Peter's blue eyes turned liquid.

"And Katie?"

"We'll see. Let's work at it. Let her get to know you a while longer as just my friend. We'll see."

"You know how hard this is for me. Seeing Katie . . . simply as her mother's friend."

"I know. It's been hard for all three of us. But Katie has an image of a daddy that might be a little hard to top right now. When she's ready for a real, live daddy with real, live faults . . . and when *you're* ready, then we'll know what to do."

"Okay. Fair enough." Peter kissed Jane again, then slowly withdrew.

"Yes, well. That was nice." Jane drew a deep breath. "But if we're finished talking I think I'll get back to what I was doing." Peter laughed. It was a beginning—something for the Irish in him to grasp.

CHAPTER 12

The Spinning of Magic

THE MANTEL CLOCK struck five. The afternoon crept towards evening and the snow still fell, softly now, lacking the intensity of the earlier storm. Things seemed to be quieting. Jane worked with her mother, trying to prepare a dinner for nine without help from the others, but just as glad to be alone. They whispered and joked, sharing gallows humor as they moved in and out of the kitchen and pantry, reaching in and out of drawers and cabinets, setting out the basics, checking on the things in the oven. For no particular reason Jane suddenly stopped, turned, and stared at her mother.

"Are you thinking what I'm thinking?" They had always read each other's thoughts. Helen had lost her sight when Jane was a teenager and, since that time, their ability to pick each other's brains had become uncanny.

"You know I am," Helen said. She leaned against the kitchen sink. For an instant she seemed to lose her balance. Jane started forward. Helen sensed Jane's movement, caught herself, and motioned Jane away. "I'm okay. It's just hard to think of leaving a place I've known since," Helen paused to place dates, "well, since James Whittlesworth Ash introduced me to his parents here

101

and John Joseph Ash and I were engaged to be married. . . ." Helen's tears began in precise drops, then increased in flow as she raised the edges of her apron to her eyes.

"I know, Mother." Jane's arms surrounded her. "I know. Even though I've been away I feel it. I felt it in Boston. I've felt it these past months. I keep trying to convince myself that this is just a big house, but I'm wrong. It's a home."

Helen started to speak, then lost her voice in short flutters of breath. For several seconds they held their embrace, daughter and mother, caught in another stage of homecoming months after the actual event.

"Maybe Uncle Whittlesworth *can* help." Jane's voice was edged with resolve.

"Bless you, Jane, you're sounding like Peter again!"

"I suppose so, but don't tag me as an urban guerrilla just yet. I just think Whittlesworth could help if he wanted to. I mean, after all this was *his* home, too."

Helen's lips drew tight. Jane knew that she was puzzling over something.

"What is it?"

"Nothing. Just something crazy."

"Whatever it is, it couldn't be any crazier than everything else going on around her lately."

"I don't know. This is pretty crazy." Helen wondered for an instant whether to speak her mind. "Jane, I'm not sure that the man out there with Katie *is* Whit Ash."

"What!" Jane's exclamation sounded like an alarm.

"Something wrong?" Sally's half-hearted voice wafted from the den.

"Nothing. Everything's fine," Jane called. Silence. Sally would never have gotten up to check anyway.

"It's not anything I'm certain about at all. And it's been almost fifty-five years. More than half a century is a long time to remember anything."

"But not the first man who kissed you."

"That's right, Jane."

"So?"

"Well, this man's voice is lower."

"He's almost fifty-five years older."

"I know. I know. But he's less courtly than Whit Ash was. Rough around the edges."

"Okay. That's enough for me. I'm going to call the police."

"No." Helen grasped her daughter's hand. "Wait. Please. I'm not certain. There are other things about him. Very important things that are just like Whit. And it's been so long."

"Well . . . okay. But you need to let me know soon. If this man is an imposter, there's no telling what's happened to Uncle Whittlesworth."

"I know. I know. Just give me some more time. Give me until tonight."

Whittlesworth's eyes began to sting. He had been reading steadily for more than half an hour and, unaccustomed to reading anything more than an occasional newspaper, let alone Christmas stories, his eyes needed a rest. He massaged the bridge of his nose while Katie snuggled even closer into his shoulder. Slowly over the past several minutes he had felt this little girl let go of her own big burdens and get caught up with the tales of other boys and girls and their parents at Christmastime. Whittlesworth marked the page with a match cover.

"Let's read some more later, Katie."

"Okay," she sighed. She was contented, at peace. Her emotions flip-flopped again. Maybe this man *was* just like her granddad.

"Well, what would you like to do?" he asked.

"Anything *you* want to do. You're Uncle Whittlesworth!" Her simple pronouncement was supremely empowering. He was the wealthy, wandering uncle come home to feast. He could indeed do anything he wanted to do.

Thaddeus appeared at the door. He had been listening from the other room, chafing over Thad Jr.'s and Sadie's failure to take advantage of Whittlesworth's potential generosity, not to mention their failure to reflect well on himself as their father.

"How 'bout coming in with us to watch the football game?"

Whittlesworth glanced at Katie from the corner of his eye. She was not impressed. Neither was he. His hours spent watching the television during an entire lifetime were few and unmemorable. He noticed the upright piano in the corner of the parlor, its keyboard covered, its bench dusty.

"Does that work?" Whittlesworth asked.

"That?" Thaddeus pointed to the piano as if he might have difficulty describing what "that" was.

"Yes, that! Does anyone play the piano in this family?"

"Well, yes. Sally's really quite good. But . . . "

"Good." Whittlesworth reminded himself that he was, after all, *Uncle* Whittlesworth. "Let's get her in here and see if she'd like to lead us in some Christmas carols."

"Christmas carols?" Piano. Christmas carols. They were like foreign terms to Thaddeus.

"Is there an echo around here? Any problem with singing some Christmas carols?"

"No. No, not at all. Just a second." Thaddeus turned and left the room crying for help. "Sally . . . Sally . . . kids . . . everybody. We're going to sing Christmas carols." There were immediate, audible groans, then Sally's voice, precise and cutting.

"I am *not* going to play the piano!"

Whittlesworth was not supposed to hear Thaddeus's hushed retort, but he did.

"Do you want this Plan or not?"

Whittlesworth whispered in Katie's ear, "This isn't going to be easy. But if you help me, I think it will work. They'll at least cooperate. For a while. Then we're on our own."

"Tell me what to do." Katie was an eager corporal.

"Okay. First, go get Peter. I'll bet he can build a fire in here. Warm this old room up a little."

"You bet."

"Then go get your mother. We need a good smoky alto. And after that, see if you can dig out some old sheet music for us. I don't want to give Mrs. Sally Ash an excuse not to play." Whittlesworth winked. She started to slip down from his lap, but Whittlesworth held her around the waist for a second longer. "By the way, you make a great reading partner, Katie." Katie hugged him, then disappeared.

Sally and Whittlesworth struck a tenuous truce. Thaddeus willingly served as truant officer over his errant children. Peter finished building the fire, then joined Jane and Helen by the piano. Katie grafted herself to Whittlesworth's side. And they sang.

At first the harmony of their voices and their movements sprang strictly from necessity. No one wanted to anger Uncle Whittlesworth. Their reasons might differ slightly, but their goal was the same. So they sang together. No one ran for the television or the telephone. No one argued about the Plan. No one even mentioned the next morning's meeting. For a while they acted like a family.

Then gradually, while they sang "The First Noel," "Silent Night," and even "Jingle Bells," something happened. They ceased to just act like a family, and they started to actually function like one. It began with a healthy airing of their lungs, not with harsh words or anger, but with the simple exercise of singing. Air in. Air out. Then came the laughter—a wrong note or two from Sally, followed by a reassuring hand from Whittlesworth. An astounding ignorance about the words to the Christmas carols exhibited by Sadie and Thad Jr., forgiven by all with the sentiment that it was the thought and not the performance that counted. Subtle tickling of both Katie and Jane by Peter's sneaking fingers, returned in kind by Katie. Laughter flowed from one moment to another, passing from one family member to another.

Though Helen couldn't see them, she sensed their joy, and she laughed until her sides ached. Whittlesworth turned around and gave her a peck on the cheek. Everything faded together into the magic of a snowy afternoon. Whittlesworth smiled as he heard their voices improving by the fifth song. They were learning to sing together—like the challenge he had given to his homeless compatriots just the night before.

Whittlesworth's present challenge was what to do next. If he stopped, they might lose momentum. He didn't want to return to the isolation of the early afternoon. If he led them in singing much longer, he was going to run out of songs to suggest. And so, with a question here and a wink there, a solicitation of their favorites and an occasional cessation of singing by himself, he slowly turned the show over to them. Soon they were calling out the names of tunes, and when they did he would scurry through Helen's yellowed and dog-eared book of Perry Como's favorite carols to find them, acting as their servant as well as their master.

As minutes turned into an hour, the most remarkable change of all was that the peace between Sally and Whittlesworth became genuine rather than tenuous. The more he praised her playing, the closer she edged towards him. She was melting. They were all melting.

Whittlesworth felt the nudge of Jane's shoulder as she peeked over his shoulder to see what the next song would be. He turned and looked into her eyes. In some ways she was even a greater challenge than Sally. A woman wronged by the world—a thoughtful, feeling woman who was unable to shed the immense chip she had placed on her shoulder through the years.

"Jane, you must have been a daddy's girl at some time or other. You remember John's favorite, don't you?" He was taking a chance that she'd have to ask him.

Jane blushed, then lowered her head, embarrassed. She looked to Peter for help, but he merely smiled and tightened his hold on her shoulder.

"Good King Whittlesworth." Jane giggled like a little girl. "I mean, Wenceslas." Sally found the right page and they all broke into song. They sang every verse, and they were still singing when the buzzer went off in the kitchen. Sally lifted her fingers from the piano and begged for a rest. Helen excused herself, patting Whittlesworth lightly on the shoulder. Jane followed her mother, and Peter followed Jane.

Whittlesworth stood up from the bench, thanked Sally in chivalric terms which surprised himself even more than Sally, then moved to the fire. He poked at it until it glowed, then he lifted one of the logs Peter had gathered and dropped it in the midst of the embers. New flames rose up. It reminded him of all the battered oil barrels beside all the shabby missions where he had taken a meal. Simple, warm, and comforting. The basics.

"Tell us about old-time Christmas." Katie's request came without warning as she plugged in the Christmas tree and turned off a table light or two. The mood softened.

Whittlesworth turned, his face silhouetted by the flickering fire-light. Jane and Peter had returned from the kitchen; it was a near capacity audience once again. If he told them too much someone might begin to ask questions. He was close to securing the fortune that was tucked away in the black satchel, nearer still to regaining his freedom. The last thing he needed was a misstatement, some item of history which was patently wrong.

"I've forgotten so much." Whittlesworth tried to turn back to the fire, excusing himself from anything more difficult than stirring logs.

"What about the first years when you ran away from home and rode the boxcars?" Jane's query was filled with childlike eagerness.

She wasn't asking for much. He wondered if Jane's Uncle Whittlesworth had actually ridden some of the same cars, during the same years as himself—and then become a millionaire many times over. Who would know the difference between the two hobos when it came to tall tales of the road?

"Okay. Sure." Whittlesworth turned the logs for maximum flame and warmth—a skill acquired over a lifetime. "Let's see, now. Okay. Well, it was right before the big war . . . "

"Just before you made your first fortune?" Jane's question seemed more probing this time. Maybe it was his imagination.

"Yes . . . about then. I don't remember exactly. Anyway, I was traveling out west on the Santa Fe line. It was Christmas, and I was with a fellow who just called himself Dub. Can't remember where he was from, although I should. You know how it is when you get old. You can't remember yesterday, but you can remember fifty years ago like it *was* yesterday.

"Well, Dub was the kind of guy who couldn't seem to finish what he started. He always had good ideas, but just couldn't follow up on 'em. When I went off to make a few bucks . . . " The room erupted in laughter. For a moment Whittlesworth didn't realize what he'd said. When he did, he joined in the laughter. "Right, well, I guess Dub kept on wanderin'. Pickin' fruit, working the carnie circuit. Always good ideas, but never could put them together. But anyway, that Christmas before the war, the winter of the Great Blizzard, they called it . . . "

Whittlesworth rambled at first, filling his tale with cold boxcars, campfires in rock crevices, pilfered meals, and railroad detectives. Then, like the steel wheels of the freight trains he boarded, his voice assumed a steady cadence. Humming with his descriptions of an untamed countryside still emerging from its rural traditions and Wild West legends, his stories of occurrences savage and cruel, meek and innocent all melded into the rhythms of the wanderer's road.

When he described the cold that he and Dub endured that Christmas, no one in the family avoided a shiver or the need to cuddle closer to something or someone. For Jane, it was Peter and Katie, the three situated on the large sofa. For Thaddeus, it was Sally, who surprised him after a few minutes of Whittlesworth's narrative by leaving her position of distance and escape by the pocket doors to join him on the arm of the wing chair next to the fire. For Thad Jr. there was one end of the smaller sofa, for Sadie the other, brother and sister enjoying a rare truce, their stockinged feet touching at the middle. When Helen rejoined them, she moved to the other wing chair, nearest Whittlesworth's post by the fire. Together they all heard the howl of northwest winds echoing down blind canyons, they warmed at the description of crackling campfires, their mouths watered at the account of the Christmas chicken—a delicacy Whittlesworth and Dub had earned for chopping wood on Christmas Eve. His adventures, his hardships, his sadness, his joy became their own.

"So we made it out of that mountain pass and down into the valley. Dub and I had almost died up in that snow. When we got to where the tracks split, he went his way, and I went mine. And we never saw each other again. That was almost fifty years ago. Dub was a friend. A good friend." Whittlesworth's words took on an eerie, almost ethereal quality. "I'd almost forgotten him. . . ."

His voice had lowered to a whisper. The room was silent except for the sharp popping of the green wood on the fire. Whittlesworth sighed. Something had happened to him as he spoke. Perhaps a combination of the fire, the warmth, the people, the attention. The feeling of family had infected him as it had them. He cleared his throat.

"Well, I could go on forever with these old stories." He paused, looking down at Helen. "And we could starve and that turkey I smell could be wasted. So why don't we eat dinner instead. Right, Helen?"

"Right, Whit." Helen turned her head in his direction. "As long as you share some more of yourself with us after dinner!" An immediate second resounded from everyone in the room, followed by a gradual stretching of relaxed limbs and a slow meandering towards the dining room.

Whittlesworth replaced the brass poker in its carriage by the mantel. Its solidity had provided comfort as he shared tales of his past with his adopted family. He began to understand for the first time what fathering was all about—the comfort and the burden of lineage, the enhancement of an individual's worth by the members of his family. Family. The word itself seemed new to him, like "home" or "roots" or any of the other alien terms which seemed to be floating through his mind. They were foreign to his past life, but no longer so fearsome. Whittlesworth chuckled as he started towards the dining room. To think that he could be some sort of godfather.

Thaddeus and Sally were waiting for him by the hallway door. Sally looped her arm within his. Thaddeus walked beside him, avoiding contact, still tentative with his suddenly incarnated older brother.

"We enjoyed your stories, Uncle Whit." Sally's appellation for him had a natural, spontaneous feel. Her well-manicured beauty was seductive, her voice saturated in sincerity.

"And your visit today has really been fine!" High praise indeed for Thaddeus.

"But please remember the meeting tomorrow morning."

"Nine o'clock sharp," Thaddeus chimed.

"We need your help. The family needs your help. You need to make the hard decisions for them."

"Sally's right, you know. It's been nice. All of these stories and singing around the piano and so on. And there's no reason it won't be just as nice tomorrow, or on Christmas day. But we can't have any more delays." Thaddeus paused. "You're a businessman. Aren't you?"

Whittlesworth read more into Thaddeus's smirk than was intended.

"What are you getting at?"

"I just mean that you know how deadly delays can be. A day, even an hour or two can kill a whole project."

"Yes. Yes, I see what you mean."

"Right." Thaddeus's voice lost its satin and softness. "I don't want any more delays. You owe that much to us. This property doesn't mean anything to you. But it's my chance to make something work. It's the family's chance for security."

"Now wait just a minute."

"No. You wait a minute." Thaddeus's tone hardened. "You like Jane. Great. She's broke. Maybe she'll get back with Peter. Fine. But he'll never provide for her. And you like Katie, too. You'd probably like to see her go to a nice school and wear decent clothes. That's fine, too. You could provide it for them directly. That would be charity. Or you can give them a chance they won't give themselves."

"I don't know that they want that chance."

"Look. You don't even have to be here tomorrow. Catch my drift? You could be sick or something. Just sign the proxy. Hell, I don't care how you do it. Just don't jump back in after all of these years and mess things up!"

"Calm down, Thad." Sally's voice was still soothing, seductive in its power. "You understand, don't you, Uncle Whit?"

"Sure. I understand." It was all that he could say. They entered the dining room and took their places. Whittlesworth's newly discovered sense of harmony dissolved. All of the caroling and warm fires and offerings of peace and good will had faded once he yielded the floor. All sacrificed in the pursuit of mammon. It was a force he couldn't fight. Resist, maybe, but not fight. His course, unclear only minutes ago, became clearer than ever: get out. Get out soon. Get out before their stupid meeting with their stupid board trapped him within a course not of his choosing. Get out before Peter or Jim Spencer tried again to shame him into an act of foolish resistance. Get out before the discovery he had been fearing somehow became a reality. Take care of number one. Save Dub, not Whittlesworth.

CHAPTER 13

Evening Rituals

WHITTLESWORTH RAISED HIS soup spoon to his lips. An uncommon aroma—a delight to his senses. A single, satisfied slurp broke the silence that had settled around the table. His eyes strained upward from his spoon, then perused the faces of his "family" circled around him. Shocked disdain was evident from Sally and Thaddeus. Bemused surprise from Peter, Jane, and Helen. Open-mouthed indifference from Thad Jr. and Sadie. A clearing of throats, intermixed with muffled laughter from all but Katie. Whittlesworth lowered his spoon. He might as well have stirred his soup with his big toe.

"I've been eating alone for so long . . . I've forgotten my manners."

There was a collective sigh, then Jane's low, soothing voice.

"Our manners are worse for staring at you."

"Katie, would you lead us in grace?" Helen shifted attention as she took Katie's hand. Katie in turn took her mother's hand, and Jane, Peter's. Peter reluctantly took Sally's elegant fingers in his, much as he would have held the legs of a tarantula. Sally shivered at Peter's touch, equally abhorrent, then grasped Sadie. Sadie reached over

111

to Thad Jr. and Thad Jr. to the hand of his father. Thaddeus started to slide his hand matter-of-factly into Whittlesworth's, then stopped. How could such a ritual be matter-of-fact? He was about to say grace with a brother he had never known nor shared grace with before. Whittlesworth, still recovering from his earlier faux pas, hadn't noticed his hesitation or the chain of hands anyway.

"Whit." Thaddeus extended his hand. Whittlesworth glanced around and realized what was occurring. His rough, knobby fingers—still thick with muscle and sinew—joined Thaddeus's, then he eased his palm into Helen's and the circle was complete.

They bowed heads and Katie began.

"God is great, God is good, and we thank him for our food—and Uncle Whittlesworth coming home." Her eyes began to open. "And I hope he stays."

"Amen," Jane said.

"Rolls." The single, grunted command came from Thad Jr. It was the first word he had spoken in over an hour. His hand was outstretched.

"Pass the rolls, please!" Sally's embarrassment was obvious. Her sixteen-year-old possessed the manners of a four-year-old. Where did such rudeness come from?

"I asked for 'em first," Thad Jr. retorted, oblivious to her lesson in decorum.

"Never mind," she muttered, promptly passing the rolls.

Soup finished, Whittlesworth began to congratulate himself on making it through the first ten minutes of dinner. Peter helped Jane clear the bowls, then they returned to the table.

"How about some turkey, Whit?" Thaddeus held the plate of sliced white meat towards him. Whittlesworth started towards the turkey with his own fork, then stopped.

"Old habits . . . living like a hermit." He grinned at Thaddeus. Whittlesworth gingerly reached for the serving fork and helped himself. The meat was tender, cooked far better than the turkey he had annually sampled at shelters around the country. Another plus on the side of home life. Stop that, he told himself. Stop the "home, sweet home" stuff. He lifted his fork to his mouth just as Jane interrupted. Something else was wrong now. The first bite was becoming a real struggle.

"I would like to offer a toast," she said. They all picked up their wine glasses. Whittlesworth took his and began to raise it. Then he heard Jane's words and he lowered it again. "To the uncle I had never seen, for all of the years he has been a mystery to us, and for the years to come when we hope he won't be a mystery anymore."

"Hear! Hear! And for the vision to see . . . " Thaddeus began, but was quickly cut off.

". . . that might is not always right!"

"Now, see here, Peter, sooner or later you're gonna . . . "

"Both of you!" Helen's voice commanded silence. "If anyone should be concerned about decisions downtown, it should be me. But I join in Jane's toast. And I'll add something: the light you have brought to us this afternoon surpasses any fire we might have expected!"

Whittlesworth slid his chair back and stood up. An involuntary action, hardly intended, but one that was compelled by an odd combination of guilt and bathos, a sudden revelation in the ordinary ritual of dinner.

"I have been all too many years away from family. And no matter where I go, or how long I may be away again, I'll always remember this brief Christmas with all of you." They all raised their glasses—except for Katie—and sipped, touched by his words. Even Thad Jr. and Sadie were aware that something special was happening. When they lowered their glasses no one seemed to know what to do. Jane was the first to speak.

"How 'bout some more wine?"

"I can get it, dear." Helen was always ready to prove her lack of disability.

"No, mother. But thank you. Peter, why don't you come on and give me a hand."

"Hmmm?"

"I said I'd like a hand." Jane gave him a quick wink, grabbed his hand, then got up and drew him into the kitchen.

Once the swinging door had closed, Peter's hands moved to Jane's waist and he drew her to him. They kissed. Peter pressed more firmly and began to draw her into his arms.

"Come on, Peter. Not now."

"Then when?"

"Open the wine while we talk."

"Okay. But what did I do wrong?"

"Nothing. We just have to talk quickly."

"Okay. But what's so urgent?"

"Well, fighting Thaddeus's Plan for one thing."

It was Peter's turn to draw back. "This is a change of position. When did you get religion?"

"I've never been on Thaddeus's side in this thing."

"But you haven't been on ours, either. You've just sat on the sidelines and thrown barbs."

"Well, maybe I wasn't committed. Now I am."

"Why?"

Jane stopped to collect her thoughts. "Family. Families sprinkled throughout this neighborhood. The fact that my family built this house and this park."

"What made you come to that realization? Lord knows I've been trying to tell you that for the past year."

Jane laughed. "That old man in there. His stories. His way with Katie."

"Uncle Whittlesworth is a real character, all right."

Jane sobered. "That's the other thing. I don't know if that *is* Uncle Whittlesworth."

"What?" Peter leaned against the kitchen wall. "What are you talking about?"

"You'd think Mother would remember the voice of her first love. If anything, blindness has heightened every other sense. Voices are like faces for Mother. But she doesn't recognize that voice."

"It's been over fifty years. A voice can change a lot in that time."

"Maybe. Maybe not. That's why I'm only telling *you*. That's why Mother isn't sure."

"What's going on in there?" It was Whittlesworth's good-natured call for their return. The wine had put a slight lilt in his voice.

"Nothing. Just having trouble with the cork. We'll be there in a minute," Jane called through the door, then returned to Peter. "I'm just saying that, among other things, with all the stuff Thaddeus is laying on him about the Plan, it wouldn't hurt if we had a few aces up our sleeve."

"I don't know if that would be right."

"You'll have to decide that. Thaddeus would use anything in his power to stop you. Sally would go a step or two farther. If something fishy's going on, I'm going to the police. But in the meantime, do you want to fight fire with fire?"

"I'll think about it." Peter's tone was somber. "But I appreciate your change of heart."

"Maybe I just found my heart."

The door to the kitchen flew inward. Thad Jr. lumbered upon them, his hand grasping the water pitcher. "I'm thirsty," he announced.

"Aren't we all?" Peter said. Thad Jr. looked at him blankly.

After dinner, when the dessert was finished and the coffee poured, the dishes cleared and stacked in the kitchen for washing later that night, the family regathered in the parlor at Katie's insistence. If it hadn't been for Katie they would have scattered, some to the television, others to the kitchen, some to the parlor to look at the afternoon paper. The mood of the afternoon still lingered, but in the fashion of adults, they were too self-conscious to tell each other what they wanted to do.

It took the child in their midst to achieve what they couldn't. Katie had grabbed Uncle Whittlesworth's hand and announced to the others that storytime would resume. Whittlesworth didn't deny her claim, so no one raised a word in protest. This time he sat in the wing chair, Katie on his lap. Chairs and sofas were drawn closer, and the fire rekindled. It was seven thirty when he started and almost nine thirty when he finished.

". . . and so I rode that train alone that Christmas just before the war, mourning the loss of that old dog that had traveled with me for five years. I knew that he was as close to family as I was likely to know again. It snowed ten inches out on the plains, from Topeka to Denver. Then it snowed another two feet. It snowed and never seemed to stop. Eventually it buried my sadness in its drifts. But you know, it's funny. Here I am now, and I can almost feel his warmth around me in this room. Strange, isn't it?"

No one laughed. There were a few sighs, one or two soft murmurs of assent, a quick breath signifying restrained emotion—substitutes for more direct expressions. Katie was the first to speak.

"Tell us more. Tell us how you built planes in World War II." Whittlesworth felt the now familiar twinge of fear. Always a reminder, even from the youngest and least threatening, that his own past could never supplant the past of the man whose place he had taken.

Jane saved him. "Enough, Katie. Time for you to go to bed. Tomorrow's a big day."

"Please, Mommy."

Jane smiled at her skillful pleading. "No. Now, grab my hand and up we go. . . ."

"I'll take her up." Peter's eyes met Jane's squarely. "If it's okay with you."

Jane started to say no, to quickly interpose herself protectively between Peter and Katie. To pour forth the litanies that had become second nature. Then she stopped. It was a night to reconsider such things.

"All right. But she has to brush her teeth first."

"And can Uncle Whittlesworth read to me when I get into bed?"

Jane marveled at her daughter's ability to manipulate the situation to her whims.

"Yes. If Uncle Whittlesworth wants to read to you." Whittlesworth smiled and nodded. He would appreciate some more time alone with Katie, away from the dangers of the adults. "But not too long. Choose something short."

"All right," Katie said, triumphant. Peter offered his back and she jumped on him. First she said goodnight to Thaddeus and his family, then she kissed Helen goodnight. Jane promised to be up after her story. Peter turned and like horse and rider they bounded up the stairs.

"We need to be on our way," Sally announced. Thaddeus agreed, and together they began the process of collecting coats and saying their goodbyes.

Whittlesworth remained seated, debating whether he would call Buddy after all. Perhaps he could get through another day or two. Go along with Thaddeus and his board and ease the transition for Katie and Jane and Helen. He stared into the fire, wondering if this conglomeration of strangers could provide his final resting place after a lifetime of wandering. No, that wouldn't be possible. Too many risks. But for a day or two, a week at most, it might be possible. Enough to stockpile some memories for the few years he had left.

"We'll see you tomorrow morning," Thaddeus noted softly at his side.

"Yes. Yes. Of course."

"I'll be by around 8:30."

"Yes."

"You'll remember what we said earlier?" Sally stated more than asked.

"Yes. Of course I will."

A few moments more were spent in goodnight wishes and thank yous. Then Thaddeus, Sally, Thad Jr., and Sadie were gone. Jane returned to the kitchen, tired of playing hostess and maid, but satisfied that Peter would be down to help Helen and herself in a minute.

Finally alone, Whittlesworth poked the fire one last time. He stabbed a glowing log and it splintered in a shower of red and yellow shards. Thaddeus's final words plagued him. Whittlesworth was still simply a puppet in the entire process. The realization made him angry.

"Katie's in bed, Mr. Ash."

Peter startled him. Twenty-four hours of domestication and he was getting sloppy, daydreaming when he should be alert. Whittlesworth wheeled around with the poker in his hand, for a moment a creature reacting to its raw need and instinct to survive. For a moment he was again the man who had fought when he needed to defend himself, wielding two-by-fours or tobacco stakes or iron rods, growls emitting from his throat to scare his attackers away, separated only by a shadow from his animal cousins.

"You caught me napping." Whittlesworth slowly lowered the poker. "Sorry."

"Uh . . . no problem. I just wanted to tell you that Katie's in bed. She's . . . ready for a story."

"Right. I'll go on up."

"Mr. Ash?"

"Yes."

"I just wanted to share something with you. About Helen."

"Yes?" There was an edge to Peter's voice. Another surprise was in the offing.

"It's just that when she heard your voice, she, uh . . . "

"Yes. She what?"

Peter knew the next lines in his script—the hushed tone, the knowing smile, maybe even the hint of a wink that said, "I know something that you don't want anyone else to know, but we can keep it between us. Just play the game and no one needs to know." Jane had made this moment of opportunity available to him. The delivery needn't be polished, nor the words carefully selected. All that was required was a harmless anecdote to let the old man know he was suspicious. The veiled offer of a compromise would follow. Similar things had been practiced on Peter many times in the professional world—and they made him sick.

"When she heard your voice and felt your touch, she said hundreds of old memories came back to her. You've made her very happy."

Whittlesworth peered into his face, trying to read the unannounced truths which it might reveal.

"Thank you, Peter."

"Helen feels the same way Jane and I feel. We know you'll do the right thing tomorrow morning."

"Thank you again. Now, I'd better see Katie before she falls asleep."

"Yes, of course."

Whittlesworth left the room knowing that Peter was holding something back. Written on Peter's strained smile, unspoken but present on his tongue, suppressed in his silent thoughts—Peter knew about him. Exactly what Peter knew and to what extent it spelled danger for him he could only guess. He didn't want to guess. Whittlesworth was sick of the tension, the gamesmanship, the curbed tongue. He wanted out.

He climbed the stairs to Katie's room. She was beneath the covers, staring at the ceiling.

"Hello, Katie. Know what you want me to read?"

"Yes."

"Okay. Where is it?"

Katie reached beneath her pillow and extracted a soiled cloth edition of *A Christmas Carol*. She held it towards him. He took it and sat on the edge of her bed.

"Hmmm." Whittlesworth glanced at the print. "This looks kind of grown up for a little girl." The pages flipped to the fly leaf and he saw a child's handwriting. He read the inscription out loud. "To my little brother John, from Whit. Friends and Brothers True. Merry Christmas, 1929." He looked at Katie. Her face was like a single dot of light in a sky devoid of stars and moon. There was no doubt in her mind, no ambiguity to her universe. In that place he was infallible, godlike.

"That was a long time ago, Katie."

"Grandpa read the last chapter to me the night before he died. Don't read it if you're going to die." Her smile had faded.

"I think I can test fate that far, Katie. But if I croak, don't ask anybody else to read."

"Croak?"

"Never mind. It was a joke. An old person's joke. Now, let's see here." Whittlesworth began to read. He was still out of practice, but was not without facility. "'The End of It,'" he began, "'Yes! and the bedpost was his own. The bed was his own, the room was his own. Best and happiest of all, the Time before him was his own, to make amends in!'" Whittlesworth read on, gauging from time to time whether Katie was dozing off to sleep. She watched him throughout. He simultaneously felt self-conscious and self-important. Time passed, until he finally reached the end.

"... and it was always said of him that he knew how to keep Christmas well, if any man alive possessed the knowledge. May that be truly said of us, and all of us! And so, as Tiny Tim observed, God Bless us, every one!"

Katie reached forward and gave him a hug. A second passed before he extended his own arms around her fragile trunk. Like the gates of an opening lock, his arms seemed to invite the flow of her needs, her dreams, and her love. He could feel large, blurring tears forming in his eyes. He forced them back.

"Darling, I wish your Grandpa were still alive—but he's not. I'm not him, and I'm not much of a stand-in. I know what you're thinking . . . "

"What?"

"You're thinking that I've come back like some Santa Claus or something, and I'm gonna save your house and make your mama happy, and your grandma safe and secure, and maybe even find a place for Peter in all of this. Well, I've got to tell you something. And it's not easy. But I can't change things. I'd love to, but that's just not how it is. See?"

He could see from Katie's expression that she didn't believe in his professed fallibility. "I love you, Uncle Whittlesworth."

Whittlesworth gathered her up more tightly in his arms. So much misplaced faith. So much misguided love.

"You remember that," he said, "when it's not Christmas anymore. You remember that. And I will too, honey. I will, too."

Katie collapsed into her soft bedding. "Goodnight, Uncle Whittlesworth."

"Good night, little princess. Your mommy will be up for prayers in a second." He got up and started for the door. "Remember me, will you?" Whittlesworth pointed upwards to heaven. "I may need it."

Whittlesworth reached the top of the stairway. Jane was in the hallway below, starting up. She looked at him and smiled.

"Katie's all tucked in and ready," he said.

They started towards each other on the stair and met halfway.

"Your being here really means a lot to her."

"She's a nice little girl."

"Since Dad died last year. . ." Jane tried but couldn't find the words to complete her sentence.

"I know. It's tough to lose a mom or dad . . . grandparent, whatever."

"I'm glad you're here." She hesitated a moment, then leaned forward and kissed him on the cheek. Nothing would be easy, no parting would be simple.

"Thanks . . . it's been nice. Well, I think I'll get a glass of milk or something." Whittlesworth slid past her, heading for the kitchen.

The overhead lights were off, the dinner dishes cleaned and put away. The light from the refrigerator spread over him like an odd spotlight.

"Is that you, Whit?" He nearly dropped the gallon jug. He hadn't heard Helen join him.

"Hmm? Yes . . . just needed a little milk to settle the old system down. It's been a long couple of days."

"I can imagine." Her voice fell for a second, then it picked up with renewed intensity. "You must have had a hard journey."

"Journey?"

"From Colorado." Helen's voice seemed to probe.

"Oh, yes. Right. Hard trip. Right."

"And you drove the whole way alone."

"Right. Tough drive, but I stopped along the way . . . for meals and overnight . . . or whatever . . . " He was fumbling. He was too near departure now. He needed to hold his composure and get through until the morning.

"We had heard . . . that you were having some trouble with your heart." Now he imagined a dozen reasons for her questions. She was too curious—too close to basic truths.

"Well, I got over that. No trouble with the ticker now."

"Whit?"

"Yes?"

"If someone had a bad heart and made that trip . . . they could get in trouble, couldn't they?"

Whittlesworth could feel his ears flaming with the blood pounding from his chest. Maybe he should run now. Just open the side door and strike out.

"Yeah, they sure could. *If* they had a bad heart, or whatever."

"And if they got into trouble, do you think they would find help— or do you think they would be in danger?"

She knew. Helen knew. Had she known all along? Were the police in the next room awaiting his confession? Were they all waiting, like invitees to a bizarre surprise party? Or was Helen pursuing other paths? He had no choice. He had to trust her. What could he lose? He could always run. She couldn't stop him.

"I don't know, Helen." Whittlesworth's voice dropped as he tried to explain without explaining. "I think that if they got in trouble they would look for help . . . wherever they could find it. And I think they'd find it. People aren't as bad these days as everybody's saying. Only . . . if you were real sick, maybe you might be beyond help. Maybe you might not make it, or whatever. And then, maybe whoever was trying to help . . . might keep on trying . . . even if they kept muddling things up."

Helen's lips upturned in a smile. She walked up to him, almost as if her eyes were capable of sight. She reached out and touched his cheek.

"Whit . . . I'm glad you made it. I'm glad you're in good health.

John had his last heart attack on the way home from work one day. You're right. People aren't so bad. When his car just stopped in the intersection at Fourth and Main, people tried to help him. They tried to keep him alive. They rushed him to the hospital. But sometimes all the help in the world . . . is just good-intentioned. I'm glad you made it home okay."

"Yeah." He could feel his heart beginning to beat at a more normal pace. "I'm glad too, Helen. I shouldn't have stayed away for so long."

Helen patted his cheek again. "We always use 1 percent milk. Better for your cholesterol. Sleep well, Whit. See you in the morning."

Whittlesworth grasped her hand. In the darkness, Helen's image seemed to merge with an image from his past—an image of soft auburn hair. Their smiles were identical. If things had been different, who could predict what might have happened? But they weren't different.

"Okay. Well, if you'll be okay, I think I'll just slip up the back stairs and turn in."

"I'll be fine, Whit. I'll talk to you in the morning."

"Yeah." He finished his milk in one gulp, set the glass down on the sink and left her. Even if she didn't suspect anything, there were even stronger reasons to leave now. He could feel himself beginning to care for Helen and Jane and Katie. The entangling cords of family commitment were beginning to bind him.

He hurried up the back stairs and through the hallway to the guest bedroom. He started to turn the knob, then stopped. He turned around and looked up the stairs that led to the third floor. Along with the overwhelming urge to escape came the compulsion to see Katie's playroom one last time. He climbed the steep, curved stairs, trying not to let the treads squeak, then he carefully entered the children's playroom.

The lights in the alley behind the house reflected off the snow, flooding the room in pinkish tones of black and silver. The toys were silent, obedient. Whittlesworth leaned against one of the windowsills and looked out over the back yards of the neighborhood. A hodgepodge of gardens and garages, telephone poles and drooping wires—a haven for the eclectic. Geography with which he felt more affinity than all of the planned parks and sports arenas which could ever be built.

His moment was at hand—the invitation to fulfillment or the opportunity to escape. Stay and he might incur someone's anger or discovery. Leave and he might cause sorrow and disappointment.

Whittlesworth brought his fist down on the windowsill. The windows clattered in their loose frames. There really wasn't a choice. He must leave. The masquerade was over. He had gone too far too fast. Like Icarus flying towards the sun, his freedom and his life were in jeopardy every moment he flirted with the flame of family.

When things quieted down throughout the house he would find a phone where no one could hear him. "Buddy," he would begin, "we've got to move on. Meet me bright and early tomorrow morning at the Mission. We'll walk over to the rail yards and head south. Pickin's will be good in Florida. Better than you've ever dreamed." Buddy would be ready with a change of clothes, food, and a handshake. Buddy was his friend. Whittlesworth was Buddy's friend. They needed each other. He knew it was true, and yet, as he stood in the shower of snow light, the dolls and toy soldiers of three generations of children witness to his anguish, his heart ached at the decision he had made.

CHAPTER 14

Home to Stay

HE SLEPT PEACEFULLY. The soft mattress, feather pillow, and down comforter should have been foreign to him, but instead they surrounded him like a womb—at least until the dawn. The minute the gray light of a new sun permeated the clouds he was awake and resolved. Rising from the soft mattress, brushing aside the feather pillow, and thrusting back the comforter, he didn't stop to yawn or stretch. Buddy was waiting for him. Standing in some weathered doorway with a hot cup of coffee. Waiting.

He slipped on the pants and shirt, the socks and shoes, the vest and coat of the man whom he had come to know so well during the past thirty-six hours. He would know him no longer. He stuffed the tie and handkerchief in his coat pocket, picked up his bags, and slipped down the stairs. Get out. Now. Don't wait. Don't stop to look in on Katie. Don't even think of looking in on Helen. Don't think about it. Down the stairs, do what had to be done and then out the door. Disturb no one. Wake no one.

He stopped at the same secretary where Katie had penned her letter to Whittlesworth—the twin of the secretary where the old man from the West had first contemplated his letters from Katie and Thaddeus. He needed to buy time now. An hour or two. No telling when the next freight train would roll through town.

He pulled Thaddeus's letter from his coat pocket and withdrew the proxy. So this single sheet of paper could invest power in Thaddeus, the little brother. Maybe it would satisfy Thaddeus when he found that his older brother had flown the coop. All that Thaddeus had ever wanted was the carte blanche to do as he pleased with the neighborhood. Thaddeus wouldn't care where Whittlesworth had gone. There would be no police searches instigated by Thaddeus, no questions asked, no "all-points bulletins" across the country. Thaddeus would have the proxy, signed and irreversible. That would end it all. Thaddeus wouldn't try to check the signature for authenticity. He scribbled on the signature line: James Whittlesworth Ash. There. It was done. He put the document in a blank envelope and wrote Thaddeus's name on the outside. Thaddeus would pick up the proxy at 8:30 instead of picking up Whittlesworth.

He started to seal the envelope, then stopped. There had to be more—a final flourish of some type. He grabbed a pen and scribbled a note:

"Tired of business and too long away
to regain family. Gone back. Caught an early
flight. Sell the car. Do what's right."

Your brother,

Whit

He heard a creak from the floor above him. Probably just the house speaking to him. He slipped the note into the envelope for Thaddeus and sealed it. He started to scribble another note to Jane and Katie and Helen and Peter, then stopped. What could he say in the brief time he had to say it? Nothing. "Sorry, I lost my nerve?" If he wrote anything he might never leave. And he was determined to leave so that he might survive.

The sour taste of the glue made him wince. He pressed the flap closed and laid it in full view. They couldn't miss it. It was past the time to go. He took one last look around the room where for one glorious day he had been king of the clan, and the clan had been his own to embrace. The Christmas tree had been left on all night. Its tiny lights filled the parlor with multicolored radiance, reminding him more than ever that it was Christmas Eve, and that he was leaving. He grabbed up the bags, went to the enormous entrance doors, turned the lock and then the knob . . . and left. "Don't look back," he told himself.

Katie lay in her bed, staring up at the ceiling, her Christmas wishes already secure. When she had heard her Uncle Whittlesworth get up moments earlier, she imagined that he was like Santa Claus, departing silently in semi-darkness to bring joy to the less fortunate. That had to be why he had told the man on the phone he would see him at the Wayside Mission this morning. Katie hadn't meant to eavesdrop the night before, but his low-spoken words on the upstairs phone had been irresistible. When she had finally fallen asleep it was with even greater admiration for the man who had answered her letter and entered her life. At Thanksgiving and on the past three Sundays this month, her mother had taken Katie with her to the Mission to help in the kitchen. Uncle Whittlesworth must be leaving to serve breakfast to needy families, or maybe to bring them gifts on Christmas Eve morning. She never doubted him for a minute.

Uncle Whittlesworth would be back by 8:30—in time for Uncle Thaddeus to take him to the meeting. Katie started to get up. Maybe she could catch him long enough to wish him a good morning and a merry Christmas Eve. The floorboards made their familiar sound: screech-creak. No, if Uncle Whittlesworth wanted to keep his good deeds secret, that was just fine. She wouldn't say a word. She plopped back into bed. A minute later she heard the front door ease shut.

Jane rushed to the bathroom and yanked the shower curtains closed behind her. This was no morning to oversleep, yet oversleep she had. Her excuses were sound. She and Peter had sat before the fire until almost one that morning, groping with their words until they began to make sense, fabricating a future they could accept, covering the past one last time. Reviewing, analyzing, and ultimately dismissing it. They could draw from it and move on.

This morning was the beginning of their future. Jane was going to the last board meeting. She would finally fight for a heritage only Uncle Whittlesworth's presence had brought into focus. Later, Katie would receive the strangest Christmas present of all. A little confusing, perhaps, but she would come to understand. The important thing for now was to introduce Peter in his new and proper role as Katie's father. The details could wait until she was older.

Jane dried off and glanced at the fogged-over face of the digital bathroom clock. She wiped it dry with her bath towel. It was 8:15— no time for breakfast, or coffee, or even a cigarette. Jane smiled. She didn't even seem to need one. Thaddeus would surely serve coffee and Danishes to his illustrious board of the city's elite.

Peter's banging had not quite ceased when she turned off the hair dryer. She heard Helen's voice saying, "I'm coming. Hold on. Don't burst a vessel." Jane laughed. Peter *had* changed—he was finally on time.

She looked into the mirror for the final check. No pouches. No red eye. No drooping cheeks. She must have slept well. Maybe she really *was* in love. Jane put on her lipstick, eyeshadow, and liner, all in record time. "Don't mess up now," she whispered to herself. "You look good."

Jane flung open the bathroom door just as the cadence of the voices downstairs changed. She zipped up her dress and slipped on her best Boston press conference flats.

"No. No. It can't be." Peter's voice, intermixing fear and anger.

An excited torrent of words from her mother, then the sound of feet rushing from one room to the next. The front door slamming again. Thaddeus's voice boomed, and there was increased activity. Something was definitely wrong.

"Gone!" Thaddeus's unmistakable roar.

"Jane, quick, get down here now!" Peter called up the stairs.

Jane rushed past Katie's closed door, distracted by the anxiety in the voices below. Katie must be asleep still. Peter was crying out again. Jane ran down the stairs, fully aware that something very serious had happened or was still happening.

"There's no mystery about it." Peter was pacing in and out of the parlor like a crazed man. "He's gone!"

"What?" Jane ran down the remainder of the stairs and demanded an explanation.

"He's gone, Jane." Helen felt for her daughter's hand.

"Gone? What do you mean? When did he go?"

"Maybe I'd better call the police. Maybe he's had some kind of blackout or something. It's cold out there!" Peter was skipping from one rapid thought to another.

"Now, let's not overreact. He's done this all of his life. It's no different now. I think we just have to let him go."

"You're being awfully calm about this, Thad." Jane's tone was accusatory.

"He should be," Peter interrupted. "Whittlesworth signed the proxy before he left. Thad doesn't need him anymore."

"I wouldn't say that, Mr. O'Malley."

"Well, I would, Thad!" Jane grabbed Whittlesworth's note and proxy from Thaddeus's hands. "Did you have a hand in his leaving?"

"Really, Jane, that's low even for you!"

"I wouldn't put it past you—or Sally!"

"If you want to know who had a hand in his leaving, then look in the mirror, dear Jane."

"And what do you mean by that?"

"You smothered him to death. Even Katie. . ."

"Leave Katie out of this," Peter and Jane interrupted in unison.

"Okay. Then the rest of you. No wonder he's left. Close to sixty years without a family, and suddenly he's got more family than any twenty people could handle."

"Proxy or no proxy, you have to wait to have the meeting until we find out where he is." Peter was begging for time and he knew it.

"Not on your life. I'm leaving right now—proxy in hand," he said, grabbing it back from Jane. "And if I don't catch you at the meeting," Thaddeus's smile broadened into a triumphant grin, "you're welcome to join us at St. Francis's tonight."

Katie set her favorite doll aside as the voices downstairs changed from excited to angry. She had been listening for some time, but not for Peter or Thaddeus. She expected them. Their presence was no surprise. Katie's worry had begun to build when Uncle Whittlesworth didn't return from the Mission. He should have been back. She strained to hear him above the confused babble, but heard nothing. Then she heard her own name spoken by Thaddeus. A minute passed, then she heard a slamming door. Something was wrong. Something had happened to Uncle Whittlesworth.

Maybe she could help. Maybe there was something she could tell them. Maybe they didn't know where he had gone. Katie jumped up and started for the stairs.

"Mommy!" Katie cried out. She rounded the top of the stairs as Jane and Peter were halfway out the door. Jane heard her and turned around. Peter was tugging at her hand. The last thing she wanted to do was alarm Katie.

"Everything's okay, darling. We'll be back in an hour or two." Jane ended her brief farewell with a slamming door.

At first Katie was relieved. They must know where Uncle Whittlesworth was after all. Maybe they were going to pick him up. She hopped down the stairs, reassured. Then she saw her grandmother. Helen was still in shock, a handkerchief pressed against her lips.

"What's wrong, Grandma?"

Helen tried to think of something that would divert Katie from sharing her own sense of dread. She started to make up an excuse, then paused. She had never hidden things from Jane as a little girl. With one exception, she had always been truthful with Katie.

"He . . . Whit has left, Katie. He's not coming back. Ever." Helen's tears, held in check by her lace hanky, started again.

Katie ran for the door. She had to stop them. They were wrong. She knew where Uncle Whittlesworth had gone.

"Mommy . . . Mommy!" she screamed from the doorway as the VW pulled away from the curb.

"Katie, get back in here! It's cold and you don't have a coat!"

Her grandmother was right. Katie ran back in and went to grab her coat.

"Where do you think you're going?"

"I can't tell you, Grandma."

"Katie Ash, you stay right here."

"I won't be gone long." Katie had no idea how long she would be gone. She knew how to reach the Mission. It wasn't more than fifteen minutes from the house—not much farther than her school—but she knew that her grandmother would worry if she told her where she was going.

"Katie, get back in here!" Helen's voice was muted by the closing of the front door as Katie charged towards the sidewalk.

"Hurry up, Dub. That's the whistle. It'll be here any minute." For more than an hour they had hidden in the rubble of the lot next to the Mission, trying not to be seen by the Mission's staff or even their homeless peers. Dub fumbled with the buttons of the stained over-coat Buddy had picked up from the free rack at the Mission.

"This old coat's too small."

"Now you're complaining! Fine—your Mr. Ash's coat is stuffed in your bag. Pull it out and strut around in it for awhile!"

Dub laughed. Buddy had played his part well. The staff had found the body around noon the day before. Buddy had identified his friend, then cried and wandered around the hallways of the Mission looking lost and confused. "They said they'd give you a decent burial, Dub," Buddy had said soberly.

"I'm not complaining, Buddy. It just smells like somebody died in this coat!"

"Somebody did. You're dead, ain't you?" Buddy chided.

Dub waved his friend's comment away, then grinned. It had all worked out after all. He'd helped the old guy out, made some friends, had a good meal, and was one step away from freedom—freedom with cash for a change. They just needed to catch the next freight. Dub stood up.

"Okay, Buddy. Let's just stroll on down the street and don't look back. We've got a half a block and a street to cross and we're home free."

Dub started for the rail yards. The whistle of a freight sounded, just a mile away. They emerged from their urban bunker and started for the front of the Wayside Mission. They turned the corner of the low-slung, concrete-block structure, and Dub threw his palm back into Buddy's chest.

"Get back," Dub commanded. Buddy complied.

"What is it?"

"The cops . . . and that minister from St. Andrew's."

"What are they doing here?"

"I don't know. But I don't want to find out."

Dub grabbed Buddy by the sleeve and they circled around the back of the Mission. Their hearts started beating like they had two nights before, except that now the stakes were higher, the punishment greater. They scrambled over the back fence and started down the alley, Dub's hands grasping the handles of the bags. If they hurried they could still make the train. Their breathing came in short bursts. The two looked like little steam locomotives in the sub-freezing air. Their muscles were straining by the time they crossed the street and entered the rail yards.

Buddy stumbled. Dub picked him up.

"Come on. We're going to make it. I can hear it coming."

"I hear two of 'em coming!" Buddy said. Dub listened. Buddy was right. A freight was coming from each direction—north and south. All the better. It might make it harder to jump aboard an open boxcar, but the passing of the one train by the other might set up a cover as well. They crossed both sets of tracks.

"Okay, behind that heap of coal," Dub said, but Buddy was already moving toward it. Buddy had performed this maneuver with him hundreds of times. Let a huge mound of coal be their cover, then wait until the freight passed close by and jump aboard the first available car. Even if they were all locked, they could ride between the cars for awhile. Sooner or later they would get a break.

Dub pressed against the black pyramid of coal and looked back across the yard and the street. The cop was standing with Jim Spencer outside of the Mission. A small crowd of panhandlers was gathered around them. Their hands all flailed upward in animated discussion. Dub could only imagine what they were talking about. The train heading south, the closer one, would pass them first. They couldn't even see the northbound yet.

"Okay, Buddy. She'll be here in less than a minute."

The two crouched down. They couldn't afford to be seen by the engineer or the fireman. Once past them they would be safe. It would be a light crew on Christmas Eve. The engine rumbled past them.

Dub looked back one last time. In a matter of minutes the entire episode would simply be campfire talk—something to share over a flaming barrel at another mission in another city.

The first ten cars rumbled past, sparks shooting up from the steel rails. Dub saw a car approaching that looked like its door was open just enough to permit their entry. He firmed up his grip on the black bag that held their future. Buddy still didn't know. He would tell him once they were out of town.

"Okay, Buddy. This next one's it." Dub took a short run beside the targeted boxcar and reached out for an iron rung, his two bags clenched in his free hand. Suddenly his hand slipped with a wrenching of his wrist. The rails seemed to draw at his feet, sucking him towards them. He was going to go under. He could feel it. The two bags dropped as he waited for death. Then as quickly as he felt himself falling beneath the wheels, he felt Buddy's arms pushing him upwards. He grasped for the rungs again with both hands and held on tight. For another moment he ran beside the train, then with a loud grunt he pulled himself upward and into the car. Seconds later Buddy tossed the fallen bags to him, then followed with apparent ease.

"Close one, Dub."

"Too close," he wheezed.

"You can relax now. There they stand, still scratching their heads!" Buddy was laughing, pointing out the other open door towards the small conclave outside of the Mission. But Dub hadn't heard Buddy.

A little girl was sloshing through the snow-covered sidewalks that led to the Mission. Dub and Buddy were actually approaching her as the freight train rumbled slowly southward. Dub squinted, confirming that it was Katie who was heading towards the Mission, trudging beside the rail yard even as Dub and Buddy were leaving it. "Don't look this way, darling. Eyes straight ahead. Get with Mr. Spencer and he'll get you back home." Even as Dub formed his thoughts, it was as if Katie had read them. She turned and looked at the boxcar moving south not a hundred feet away.

"Uncle Whittlesworth! Uncle Whittlesworth!"

Even over the slow clatter of steel on steel Dub and Buddy heard her.

"Duck down. Duck down. She'll see you!"

"She's already seen me." Dub stood in the door, torn by emotions he could neither describe nor understand.

"So have our friends." Buddy was pointing towards the Mission. Spencer and the police officer had heard Katie's cry and they were already running across the street towards her.

She didn't see them. Her eyes riveted on Dub. An instant's hesitation, and then Katie started running for the boxcar. She could never catch it, but she thought she could. Dub started to lean out the door.

"Get back in here, you old fool!" Buddy grabbed at him.

A whistle blasted from his right. Dub jerked his head around and saw the oncoming northbound freight.

"Get back, Katie." His voice seemed faint and whispery. "Get back!" he screamed. She kept coming. Dub felt Buddy's hand grasping him.

"She's gonna be okay. She's gonna be okay."

Dub knew better. He knew trains and he knew tracks and he knew the kind of accidents that still happened every day in rail yards everywhere. He knew she would cross the path of the northbound freight to try to reach him on the southbound.

"Here." He hurriedly reached into the black satchel and pulled out a neatly bound bundle of money. "With all my blessings, Buddy. Merry Christmas." His last words were spoken as he clutched the bags and jumped down from the train. He landed and lost his hold on them. The smaller, black bag rolled towards the rails. For an instant he thought about retrieving it, then he gave up and lurched towards Katie. The northbound couldn't be more than a hundred feet away. Too late to stop even if they saw her. He pumped his legs as fast as they would go, crossing the parallel track ten feet before she reached it. The northbound rumbled past behind them, its horn splitting the air.

Katie rushed into his arms, his odoriferous coat quilting her as he staggered and almost fell, grasping her in thanksgiving. It didn't matter. Nothing did. Let them lock him up. She was safe. Katie was all right. They held onto each other until an intruding voice rang out above the noise of the trains.

"I don't know who you are, but you're under arrest." The voice had a familiar, slightly whining intonation, matching the young, undershaven face. Sergeant Harter was back on duty. "You have the right to remain silent. Anything you say may be held against you . . . "

"Just a minute, officer." Harter turned to face the interrupting presence of Jim Spencer by his side. "I certainly don't mean to obstruct justice or interfere with your investigation, but this man is James Whittlesworth Ash."

"That's what you say," Harter interjected.

"That's what I say, too." Katie turned and looked up at Sergeant Harter through glistening eyes and with a set jaw.

Harter stepped back and placed his hands on his hips. He had been undone once before. He had no desire to be undone again.

"I'm sorry, Mr. Spencer, and I'm sorry for you, too, little girl, but I saw this man two nights ago in an alley. He was running away from the scene of a crime."

"Excuse me, officer, but did you arrest anyone for that crime you were talking about?" Whittlesworth got up from where he had been kneeling beside Katie.

"Well, yes, we did. Two young men were detained and questioned."

"And did they confess to burglarizing that store?"

"Well, yes they did, but . . . "

"Okay. I admit that I was walking the alley near my family's home. I'd been away for a long time and I was a little nervous about going back after all of these years. I was with a very old friend from my rail-riding days. We saw the two young men robbing the store and we stopped them from getting away. You do remember that they were spread out on the pavement when you and your partner came down the alley?"

"Yes, but you were running away, too."

"My friend was frightened. He's a homeless fellow and he's a little scared at the sight of the police. I was trying to stop him."

"Well," Harter paused, trying to decide on his next tack, "that still doesn't mean you're who you say you are."

"Excuse me again, officer," Jim Spencer's delivery was soft and pastoral, "but I say this gentleman is James Whittlesworth Ash, and this little girl—who *is* his great niece—says that he's James Whittlesworth Ash. What proof do you have that he isn't?"

"Okay. Okay. Okay." Harter bore his frustration poorly. "So how come you were down here jumping on trains?"

Katie and Jim Spencer both looked to Whittlesworth. They were powerless to help him past that inquiry. Whittlesworth looked at Katie, Sergeant Harter, and then at the bags lying across the now clear tracks.

"To tell you the truth, officer, I was running away from home—just like I did over fifty years ago. And for some of the same reasons. Only it took this little girl," Whittlesworth slipped his arm around Katie's shoulder, "my great niece, to show me that this time I couldn't run away again. This time I'm home to stay."

CHAPTER 15

In Keeping with the Plan

"I'VE GOT A flight out at eleven. Let's get this going, Thad." Don Cartwright buttoned, then unbuttoned, then rebuttoned his double-breasted suit coat. Fidgeted. Time had been lost. An entire day wasted for an old man who had flown back to Denver. Cartwright tugged at his tie, gray and black amoebae jumping from their silky sea as the overhead lights shimmered across his chest.

"Okay, Don. That's reasonable." Thaddeus scooted over to the oak doors of the conference room, closed them tightly, and lowered the massive brass handle. He turned and rubbed his hands in anticipation. A disgruntled and short-tempered Board of Ash Square Development stared back in un-Christmaslike disdain.

"I move we dispense with any further formalities and approve the Plan as recommended by Cartwright and Associates." Sally's voice was pure satin, her body taut in her most businesslike black suit and pearls. She leaned forward, her red-nailed fingers scuttling across the high-gloss finish of the walnut conference table. "We've wasted enough time in discussion."

"I second Sally's motion." Frank Grissle grinned in anticipation of his daughter's moment of triumph.

"It's about time." The bishop folded his hands, then ground his palms together. "I've got a sermon to touch up."

"Okay, then," Thaddeus took a deep breath, "all in favor say 'aye.'"

"Now, wait a minute, Thad." Peter O'Malley stood up from his spot next to Jane. "I think we should at least discuss once and for all the impact Cartwright's Plan is going to have on the neighborhood."

"Damn it!" the Mayor slammed his hand down on the table, its vibrations felt by everyone. "We've talked this thing to death. Let's get on with it."

"Do it quick so it doesn't hurt?" Jane stood up beside Peter.

"You're out of order, Jane!" Thaddeus bellowed.

"And you're out of line, Thaddeus! What you're doing here is wrong!"

"Do these people have standing?" Cartwright's low and perfectly modulated voice was colder than the winds howling outside of the conference room windows.

"Come on, everybody." Peter searched the faces of the board for even a glimmer of an alliance. "Think of what you're about to do. It's not just old buildings you're talking about reducing to rubble. It's the character of the city—your city. Our city."

"And a better city it'll be built up and developed for a modern age." Mrs. Albertson turned to Ed Beech, legal counsel, who immediately nodded his assent.

"No. No. No. Don't you see? You think this fellow, Mr. Cartwright, is here to save your downtown?" Peter pointed an accusing finger at Cartwright, who met the gesture with a sneer. "He's here to build an office tower, a parking lot, and a shopping center. Straight out of standard pattern, Grade B, anywhere, U.S.A. He doesn't care if it's here . . . or in China! He cares about square-footage costs and rent and short-term leases. Make a quick buck and be gone."

"Now, see here . . . " Thaddeus's attempt to regain the floor was overcome by Peter's zeal.

"No, you see. You should all see. When this city gets ready to do something really unique with its future, we will have torn down a significant part of our past. And we'll be stuck with a bunch of ordinary glass and concrete. And Mr. Cartwright will be in Houston."

"Thaddeus, this is enough." Sally's brow arched in an unspoken command. She sensed that Cartwright was beginning to lose patience with the onslaught. Thaddeus grit his teeth and let Peter continue.

"No, Sally, it's not enough. You need to hear it all—at least once— 'cause when it's all down on the ground, and the developers clear out, there won't be any going back. Our city won't have anything unique to show off, and what we do have will be a cheap knock-off of the big cities' best. You'll have killed a part of this city that is better than the big cities—something you can't plan, or develop, or rebuild."

"So help me, Peter O'Malley, you'll never get another contract for work in this city!" Sally's lower jaw flexed in and out with her barely contained anger.

"How are you going to silence me, Sally?" Jane leaned across the table towards Sally's constricted face. "I'll go back to work with words if I have to start my own paper," Jane's glance turned quickly to Mrs. Albertson, "and I'll see that somebody calls it like it is in this city."

"Jane," Thaddeus sounded weary but resolved, "say what you will, I've got Whittlesworth's signature on the proxy, and that's all we need."

"I can make a difference, Thaddeus. You can make a difference."

"No, Jane." There was an almost sympathetic twinge in Thaddeus's voice. "Only Whittlesworth could have made a difference, and now it's too late."

"You're wrong there, brother." The deep, gravelly voice emitted from the now open doors of the conference room. Immediate silence. Whittlesworth walked calmly to the conference table with Katie's hand in his, Jim Spencer firmly planted by his side. "We can all make a difference. We all have choices still."

"But I have your proxy!"

Whittlesworth snatched the document like a falcon would a field mouse. He held it upwards for the entire board to see. "And I take back my proxy." He tore the paper in quarters and threw it on the table. "As I was saying, we all have choices." Whittlesworth's stare bored into the eyes of everyone around the table. "The first choice is whether you have a development or not. If I go along with it, you do." He paused. "And if I don't go along with it, you don't."

"Now, wait just a minute, Mr. Ash." The mayor rose to speak but Whittlesworth cut him off. He had already confronted the mayor's four children. They were more formidable than their father.

"No, you wait, Mr. Mayor. Either your citizens are going to get a facelift on their homes—along with St. Andrew's Church, Mr. Bishop—or they don't get anything." Whittlesworth went around the room, addressing each board member. "Either your union members get some nice, high-paying jobs, or they continue to hang around the union hall looking like the guys down at the Wayside Mission. Either your bank, Mr. Grissle, starts loaning money to some of the people who need it, or there won't be any loans to make. . . ."

"And Mr. Cartwright, either your team plays ball with the locals— namely my man O'Malley here—or the game is over right now."

Sally started to rise up slowly from her chair. "You . . . insane . . . old man."

Whittlesworth's confident smile slowly faded into a mask of steel as he turned to Thaddeus. "Thad, tell your wife to please sit down and shut up."

Thaddeus looked first at Whittlesworth, then at Sally. "Sally," he said, "you . . . are . . . out . . . of . . . order."

Sally Grissle Ash, who respected only her father's will more than her own, opened her mouth, took a breath, and fell silent. She sank back in her seat, stunned. Thaddeus smiled in spite of himself. Finally, equal footing with the woman he loved.

"Now," Whittlesworth resumed, "I'm sure Peter's plan needs some work. Maybe some more parking, some compromise here and there. Maybe there's even space for another one of your towers, Mr. Cartwright, as long as it fits in with the neighborhood. But Mr. Cartwright," Whittlesworth glanced at the artist's rendering at the end of the table, met Cartwright's eyes with his own, and locked into focus, "your architect stinks. You get a better body down here. Your *best* body—and they can work with my man O'Malley. Are we agreed?"

Thaddeus hardly knew what was happening, but he at least knew that he wasn't sure of his elderly brother's last move. He started to lean towards Whittlesworth with a word of caution, but Whittlesworth laid his hand gently on Thaddeus's shoulder and quieted him. Five never-ending seconds passed, and Cartwright stood slowly up from his seat. His expression hadn't changed—but neither had Whittlesworth's.

"I've been wondering if I'd ever find someone with guts in this town. Your reputation from the Wild West fits you well, Mr. Ash. Here's my hand on a new plan in line with your man O'Malley and the very *best* Cartwright and Associates has to offer. I think we could turn this Plan into a nifty preservation project . . . "

"And not displace everyone in the neighborhood?" Jim Spencer queried.

"Of course not, Reverend Spencer. That wouldn't be in keeping with . . . the Plan."

Whittlesworth accepted Cartwright's outstretched hand. "I want to see it in writing the day after Christmas."

"But of course, Mr. Ash. You deserve as much."

Frank Grissle finally broke into an ear-spanning smile. "I would like to withdraw my second to my daughter's motion to approve, offer a friendly amendment to adopt the Plan as it *currently* stands, and ask Sally if she will allow her motion to be so amended."

Sally was too stunned to express anything. She managed an uncharacteristically weak, "Of course . . . whatever you say," and slumped back into her seat.

"All in favor?" Thaddeus asked. Unanimous assent went up from around the table.

"The motion carries. Meeting adjourned!"

The board instantly dispersed—no time for long goodbyes or auld lang syne. At ten o'clock on Christmas Eve morning they had more things on their minds than city development plans. Yet as they filed past Thaddeus and Whittlesworth, Jane and Peter, Katie and Jim Spencer, their smiles seemed genuine, their hand clasps energetic. When they all wished each other a "Merry Christmas," the salutation vibrated with warmth.

Sally sat at the opposite end of the boardroom, stunned, trying to factor what had occurred and how it would affect her. Don Cartwright grabbed up his flight bag and briefcase, flung his overcoat over his arm, briefly acknowledged Sally, then charged towards Whittlesworth.

"I'll tell you, Mr. Ash."

"Please, call me Whit."

"Okay, Whit. I've got to hand it to you. You're a tough cookie. You play your cards down to the wire."

Whittlesworth remembered the greasy, dog-eared cards he had cut with Buddy two nights and a thousand years before. He smiled.

"Always have, Don."

"Well, I look forward to working with you. You'll be sticking around here, right?"

Whittlesworth swiftly reviewed the cast of his still disparate family—Thaddeus, Sally, Jane, Katie and, soon, maybe even Peter. They were still in need of a helping hand, still capable of greater good for themselves and their city, still able to sing their song together as a family. They stared back—to a person, even Sally—in need of his efforts and contributions.

"Yeah, I think I'll stay. I may travel around. I've had enough of staying in one place. But I think I'll be giving up the place out West. 'Course, you'll really be dealing with my partners."

"Huh?"

"Well, Thaddeus here is going to continue to head up the show. That's if you want to, Thad."

Thaddeus smiled. No longer would Sally or Frank Grissle or anyone else wield such power over him.

"Yes," Thaddeus nodded, "I'll gladly serve with you, Whit."

"And Peter as your architect?"

"Sure . . . assuming all's forgiven?"

Peter grinned. "It's going to feel funny working with the folks on the inside for a change. But I can get used to it."

"And Jane as your wordsmith. . . ."

"If you weren't so hard to bargain with," Jane poked him, "I'd hold out for a bigger contract."

"You sure you don't want to put the little girl on the payroll or demand a sinecure for the padre?" Cartwright jibed. Whittlesworth grinned.

"Not a bad idea. They've got more common sense than all of us."

"Well," Cartwright began the circuit of shaking hands, "I've got a flight to catch. After today, I don't care if you make the family hound the project mascot! You're a strange crew to figure out. So why try?"

"Merry Christmas," Whittlesworth called out as Cartwright slipped from their presence and through the conference room doors. His voice lowered as the doors closed. "Watch him closely, Thad, and he'll be okay."

"Maybe that could be said of me, too." Sally finally approached them from her end of the table.

"Just pretend you're playing the piano most of the time," Whittlesworth noted with a fatherly nod, "and you'll be okay, Sally."

"I'll try." Sally laughed, at last, and they all joined her.

"Thad." Whittlesworth laid his hand on his younger brother's shoulder.

"Hmm?"

"Let's all the family go to church together tonight."

"Sounds good, Whit." Thaddeus paused, started to say something, and then reformed his thoughts. "I was going to say that we'd all meet out at St. Francis tonight, but the truth of the matter is that we don't spend enough Sundays there for them to miss us if we go to St. Andrew's. Would you have us, Reverend Spencer?" Jim Spencer uttered a tongue-in-cheek "Hallelujah!"

"What do you say, Whit?"

"You read my mind, brother."

"After all these years." Thaddeus shook his head. "After all these years!"

CHAPTER 16

The End of Dub

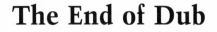

SALLY AVOIDED THE mosaic of strange faces singing to her side, her fingers picking out the familiar carol "Hark, the Herald Angels Sing."

"She's doing just fine," Whittlesworth whispered to Thaddeus as they shared a hymn book in the front pew of St. Andrew's. He sang until the end of the verse, then continued, "Glad you and Peter figured out a way to get the piano here. Wouldn'ta been as good with just Jim Spencer's guitar. . . ." Thaddeus nodded as they resumed their bellowing, ". . . glory to the newborn king. . . ."

As the carol was ending, Jim Spencer moved forward for the benediction, his eye surveying the various changes his church had experienced in the last decade: A simple piano where there had once been a grand pipe organ. A bedraggled congregation—now joined by the Ash family again—where there had once been the collective wealth of the city. A church adorned with random candlelight and chipped or missing pews where all had once been grandeur. Jim Spencer smiled. But how far it had come in just twenty-four hours! There was rediscovered hope, rekindled spirits, and renewed purpose. The music ended and he raised his hands.

"May the grace of God—which certainly surpasses *my*

understanding—be invested in all of us this glorious Christmas day. Go forth with strength of purpose and led by the guiding light of our Lord to do what is right." He nodded to Sally, she took his cue, and the strains of "The First Noel" echoed around the church.

The voices of young and old, rich and poor, weak and strong melded to one purpose. As Jim Spencer moved down the front aisle to meet people and distribute canned goods, Whittlesworth couldn't help but think back to his soap-box lecture about singing together— one song. For an instant he forgot where he was, then Katie nuzzled sleepily into his side. Helen's arm draped tightly around Katie's shoulder, while Peter and Jane nudged closely to Helen's side. Thad Jr. and Sadie stood by Thaddeus, still in shock from the circumstances that had dropped them into St. Andrew's on Christmas Eve, but also in awe of the changes in their mother, their father, and his crazy older brother. Proud members of the family whose gifts filled the windows around them.

The singing ended and they all clustered together, gathering up themselves and their winter clothes, merging with the collection of humanity that moved like a meandering stream towards the front door. Halfway there Whittlesworth separated from the family, delayed by those who wanted to meet the prodigal son and wish him thanks and a Merry Christmas. He moved slowly from one to another, still hoping that he wouldn't see any "familiar" faces. Then, just as he was breaking free, he heard the voice of someone who knew him.

"Merry Christmas, old friend."

Whittlesworth looked around, searching the faces bobbing up and down. Then he appeared, unmistakable in his old dungarees and beaten denim jacket.

"Buddy."

"I had to come back. Make sure you were okay."

They embraced, brothers and companions born of endurance and shared hardship. The stuff of all families. Whittlesworth's words failed. Seconds passed. Whittlesworth patted him on the back and then stepped back away from him, holding to Buddy's shoulders with his sinewy fingers.

"Thanks for coming back. Didn't think I'd see you again. You look great."

"You don't look so bad yourself. I've been watching you from the back. Nice family."

"Yeah. So, can you join us? I'll cover for you."

"Soon. Maybe tomorrow. Tonight I've got a hotel room. I just need some sleep. I came into some money, you know! Thought I might pay back some old debts before I lose it all."

Whittlesworth smiled. "Me, too. Need some more?"

"Not right now. You were always better with the finances." Buddy patted Whittlesworth lightly on the cheek. "Right now you need to get back and be with your family. I'll catch you later . . . " Buddy stopped short of pronouncing his name.

"Dub. I'm still your old Dub, Buddy."

Buddy pressed his lips together, exhaled, then smiled. "No. You've come home, Mr. Whittlesworth Ash. You've been a long time getting there, but I think you're home now." They clutched each other one last time, then Buddy slipped out a side door.

The congregation thinned as the ritual of goodbyes and the distribution of food and clothing concluded. A few stragglers stayed around, anxious to hear firsthand the details of the neighborhood's hopes for rebirth. Inevitably they approached Whittlesworth, reaching tentatively for his hand and responding in surprise as he urged them to acknowledge Thaddeus and Sally for their help in adopting Peter's plan. Eventually even the stragglers disappeared and the family was left alone with Jim Spencer. It was past midnight and Katie's yawns seemed to mark the passing of each second.

"Santa Claus will still come if you sleep late tomorrow, Katie." Jane patted her daughter and held her close.

"Maybe Santa Claus has already come." Katie looked at Whittlesworth knowingly, her not-so-subtle way of letting him know that he had been wrong the night before when he had denied his power to change things.

"For both of us, Katie," Whittlesworth agreed.

"For all of us," Peter whispered.

"Well, unless we intend to sleep in on Christmas morning, this family had better start for home." Helen arranged her scarf around her neck, its bright red and deep green colors giving her the appearance of Mrs. Claus.

"We'll be glad to drop you off at the house, Helen."

"Thanks, Thad. But tonight I'm feeling a little wild and crazy. If Whit will give me his arm, I think I'll walk."

"Mind if Peter and Katie and I come along?" Jane buttoned the front of her overcoat, then arranged Katie's.

"Perfectly all right. I don't know that Whit and I need a chaperone, but I think the five blocks will do us all a world of good."

Thaddeus and Sally departed with their children. Though they shared in the smiles and hugs, Thad Jr. and Sadie were still too astounded by their parents' sudden transformation to mutter more than "goodbye" and "see you tomorrow." Thaddeus left with the assurance that Jim Spencer would be joining the rest of the family for Christmas dinner, and as they fussed over time and place and who would bring dessert, Whittlesworth realized that Jim Spencer had become a member of the family as well. The door closed on Thaddeus and his family. Jim Spencer turned to those remaining in the vestibule.

"Thank you all again—for everything!"

"Thank you!" Jane's voice resounded from the walls of St. Andrew's. She laughed at her own exuberance. "If you hadn't found Uncle Whittlesworth and brought him to the last board meeting, we might all be searching for new digs in the suburbs tonight!"

Whittlesworth chafed to move along. He had been dreading any mention of the episode at the rail yards. The last thing he needed was a critical and full review of what happened.

"I still haven't gotten it straight how you knew to look for Uncle Whittlesworth down by the Mission." Peter's curiosity overcame his own common sense that some questions remain best unasked and unanswered. Whittlesworth groaned to himself, wondering what was next.

"I think I can clear things up." Helen's voice was pixilated, her smile coquettish. "When Katie tore out of the house this morning, I knew it was up to me to find her. Katie's a smart girl and she seemed to know what she was doing. I knew she wouldn't just wander off into the snow to find Whit. I figured she must have a clue to where he was. Well," she reached out and clasped Jane's hand, "call it intuition if you like, but as I was telling Jane late last evening—you remember, Jane—" Jane nodded, dumbstruck, "Whit Ash hasn't changed a bit. He's the same man who ran away from home over fifty years ago— and when he did, he chose the old freight yards as a starting place. So I called Jim Spencer and asked him to check around there." Peter and Jane's jaws simultaneously dropped.

"After Helen called me," Jim Spencer picked up the thread of her story, "I called the police. That's when Sergeant Harter got involved. He seemed certain that Mr. Ash was some sort of derelict or something." Jim Spencer's deep, resonant laugh sounded as if in a vacuum. A polite titter was all that emitted from Jane and Peter. Helen simply smiled.

"Well, I guess I'd just say that we've all been very lucky." Peter eased over towards the front door, anxious to be out and walking.

"Agreed," Jane said. "Well, goodnight, Jim."

"Merry Christmas," Spencer said. The family left and the minister closed his doors for another day.

Peter clasped Jane around the shoulders as they led the way home. Faint flurries of snow landed in their hair and stuck on Katie's out-stretched tongue. Katie slid back and forth between her mother and father walking ahead, and Whittlesworth and Helen walking a few steps behind. For all that had happened, they talked and laughed and shared passing observations as if the last two days had been the most normal in their lives.

As they neared their block, their pace slackened. They weren't eager to let these moments of triumph pass. They wanted to freeze the moment and save it—to record this stroll and remember its every detail.

Ahead, the Ash Mansion shone like a beacon, almost as if the house itself sensed its reprieve. Its light and warmth reflected in the snow, spreading out towards the rest of the neighborhood. Helen drew close to Whittlesworth, unable to see but more than able to sense their nearness to home.

"Whit," she said softly, for his ears only, "it's good to have you back home again. Sometimes, not often enough, but sometimes, things work out and old friends get a second chance."

Whittlesworth took her hand in his, realizing as he did that Katie had turned and was looking upward at them through spits of snow. Whittlesworth looked back at Katie and winked. She was the hope of the future, the light of tomorrow. Whittlesworth reached into his pocket with his free hand and felt the now crumpled letters—both Thaddeus's and Katie's—which he had kept with him through it all. For a second he looked away, back towards the Mission and the rail yards.

"Something wrong, Uncle Whittlesworth?" Katie asked.

"Not a thing, Katie, darling. Not a thing." Whittlesworth smiled. "I was just remembering an old friend who I promised I'd help get home." He tightened his grasp on Helen's arm as they turned into the gate of Ash Mansion. "I suppose he's finally there."